Oedipa Sex

A Novel

Catherine Adami

DEDICATION

To my parents, the greatest celebrities I've ever known:
Frederick Joseph Bentivegna aka "Freddy the Beard" 1940-2014
Theresa Evans Bentivegna aka "Nini" 1945-2020

To a teacher who inspired me:
"Mention sex and they'll remember everything you say."
-Dr. Marie K. Stone (1935-2005)

CONTENTS

ACKNOWLEDGMENTS

To all of my Fairy Godmothers and Godfathers, friendly ghosts, and to everyone who invested in and believes in The Pool Hustler's Daughter. Thank you.

1 EVENING

Three bourbons in, and on the wrong side of forty, Edwina "Eddy" Sass winced as she swallowed two purple pills meant to induce an uninterrupted slumber.

Eddy's sleep swung the pendulum of blood curdling screams from *paralyzing night terrors* - to deep, loud, guttural (and often embarrassing) moans from *wet dreams* that she compared to *Teutonic shifts* taking place inside of her body. Like clockwork, Eddy dreamt every night (and some might say every day) to not only escape reality but to somehow "fix" things. *Fix what*, you might ask? Oh, just her regrets, her fears, her insecurities, her *roads not taken* and every other thing which kept her feet firmly planted in cement slowly drying all around her. Everything that kept her drunk and alone at home on a Friday night, too depressed to masturbate.

Her severely repressed, *non-orgasm inducing* life was much more amplified by her impending big birthday and the death of her beloved parents. *It's now or never, motherfucker,* she giggled, inspired by Bruce Willis in **Die Hard**, a perfect example of the endless amounts of pop culture buried inside her head, as she drifted alone on her vast, empty bed, floating on the Aegean Sea without a compass. *This is my voice* she said aloud, *my real voice,* she said slowly and softly, *the real me.*

A fresh, adult orphan, Eddy thought about the next day without a homemade chocolate cake from her mother with pink buttercream flowers so carefully piped on white frosting from her decades old pastry bag, the words "Happy Birthday!" boldly written, arousing more sensitivity than usual. Eddy's arms and legs began to sink deeply into the mattress, like a giant marshmallow from Willy Wonka, and she heard her mother's voice say, *wash your face and brush your teeth before you go to bed, Princess* to which she whispered *fuck it,* and then hiccupped.

Eddy, fully dressed and lying on her back on top of her white comforter, kicked her shoes across the room, and suddenly, as her eyes began to close, she jerked upright after remembering to blow out the scented "Calm" candle on her nightstand. *I will not accidentally kill my children. I will not accidentally kill my children.*

Eddy remembered being a little girl in the 1970s and wearing her favorite pink satin nightgown, and after having a bad dream, crawling in between her parents in their ocean of a bed, while they ignored her and smoked cigarettes and watched Johnny Carson's monologue on *The Tonight Show* while reading a *People* magazine (her mother) or a spy book (her father). These two loving, vain and distracted adults had been her two best friends, whether or not they, preoccupied with their own lives, ever knew. Her parents were the stars of the show that Eddy watched rapturously, just like she had with *Sonny and Cher* and *Donny and Marie,* sitting Indian style in front of the giant living room TV holding a warm bottle of milk and her blankie.

What did she owe her parents now that they were both dead and she, Eddy, was alive?

Would she ever crawl out of the cozy comfort of a warm bed and take some risks?

Be vulnerable? *Brene Brown Brave?*

Even her father had warned her, *you have to be vulnerable to fall in love, Eddy. I fell in love with your mother because she was the most vulnerable woman I had ever met. Listen to me, I'm an expert.*

Somehow, the *I should haves* and *if onlys* that swirled in her head joined their hands together like a team of expert parachutists and dived into her chest, inducing a painful, electric, Mary Shelley scripted shock to her heart. She could hear her mother's voice, *"Darling, are you, okay?"*

With all of these *what ifs* still torturing her, could Eddy's fantasy life ever be as rich or as meaningful as her life?

Now that both of her parents – *her anchors* – were officially gone, Eddy was responsible for her own pep-talks (she was often caught talking to herself in public, so this would be nothing new), confidence and love.

Two remarkable (Eddy thought so) and smelly, loving teenagers slept in the rooms down the hall and already believed in Eddy, their mother and her talented storytelling. But, did Eddy believe in herself?

Eddy, always well liked but close to almost no one; teller of tall tales; lover of books, film, fantasy, art, music; *an imagination, that girl!*

Eddy, always brimming with childhood excitement just before her wings were clipped. A pure, perverted idealist when it came to romantic love.

Eddy, whose unanswered wish was always, always *connection.*

Eddy, who instructed her children, when they were little, to create *their own bedtime stories,* where they were *their own heroes,* who delighted in hearing them defend their higher selves with such gusto and passion before so sweetly falling asleep in her arms.

Where, then, were Eddy's bedtime stories? Where she was the hero?

There was so much she had wanted to do before this birthday, so much she had to do.

The Grandfather clock struck ten outside Eddy's bedroom just as Ira Glass's "This American Life" show began. It played on a small, analog radio that her father took with him to baseball games which she inherited along with the coveted family bagel slicer, essential to a successful Hanukkah and Christmas season.

Her father trained her to sit still and stay quiet for hours – and Eddy, like a puppy, obeyed, just to be near him. Eddy, a quiet yet screaming Genie in a bottle, entertained herself during these extended moments of silence by creating a vibrant fantasy world where she was big, bold, heroic and surrounded by celebrities and sometimes, *she was the celebrity!* In this alternate reality, she *wouldn't stop* talking – *she had a voice* – irreverent, foolish and without a filter, but definitely *brave*.

Why had she always been so afraid of speaking and acting without waiting for the approval of others? How had playing it safe actually kept her safe?

Eddy closed her eyes, wet with small tears and asked her dead, narcissistic parents for help; she wanted a second chance and to crawl out from the warm, safe but stifling, gravity blanket that she'd been hiding underneath since she was little. She wanted to wake up the next morning and say yes *to the beating heart that she had been given.*

There were so many things that she had wanted to do before her birthday. Could she get them all done in a single night? Could she wipe the slate clean and light a clear path for that connection she'd always dreamed of?

> *Que Sera, sera*
> *Whatever will be, will be*
> *The future's not ours to see*
> *Que Sera, sera*

2 BE IN PRINCE'S ENTOURAGE

By the time I arrive at Paisley Park, my fingers and toes are numb after climbing a twenty foot mound of snow over a fence and into Prince's recording compound. The wind chill is fifty degrees below zero and my thin, white, faux fur jumpsuit does nothing to keep me safe from the elements. It's Minnesota, in March.

When I reach Prince's mud room, it's cluttered with bags of salt, rubber boots and carefully separated recyclables. At least one hundred bottles of the chocolate milk drink, Yoo-hoo, in one bin. Guitar Center, Target and Ulta Beauty plastic bags in the other.

"Take your shoes off," a tall black man with a bow tie tells me.

"Are you Jerome?" I ask, wondering what I might need to pay this well-dressed, impeccably groomed man guarding the *River Styx.*

He rolls his eyes at me, and returns his attention to a crossword puzzle on his lap and sips a Red Bull.

"Take your shoes off. Prince just polished the floors."

I cautiously place my snow boots next to a pair of tiny, high heeled purple boots that make my heart race with excitement. *So close.*

Down the hall from the mud room there is a door, with hanging white beads. Behind those beads is a purple light. *I think, why not "Blue?" You know, like the song?* But it doesn't matter. *Purple light*, like a moth to the flame *I…must…go…there…*

"Where do you think you're going?" The man I know for a fact is Jerome asks. Mind you, *I've only seen Purple Rain a thousand times!*

"In…*there?*"

I point toward the beaded doorway.

"What's the password?"

"The password?"

"Yes, the password."

Still trembling from the cold and dressed in a purple satin negligee, I take a deep breath and a chance.

"What," I answer.

"What?" he asks, confused.

"The password is *what.*"

"What?"

"The password is *what!* You know, like you told Morris Day in the movie **Purple Rain**?"

"I told you *I'm not Jerome.* Are you trying to mess with me? Are you really a back-up dancer? Are you Latina?"

"Yes! I mean, *by cultural appropriation!* Didn't you see me behind JLo and Shakira at the Super Bowl Half Time Show?"

"No, I didn't. And you're definitely not Latina. Your hips…uhh…*lie..*"

I do not like the way Jerome looked at my body just then. I'm going to complain to Prince once I meet him. Does he know how many Peloton classes it took just to zip up that goddam snow suit?

"Do you even play an instrument?"

"Yes, of course, I can play an instrument. I'm a percussionist."

I start to tap my nails on *Jerome's* brand new IPAD screen. He's *not happy*.

"Do you believe in God?" he asks.

The room gets quiet. I don't want to answer incorrectly! Prince is a Jehovah's Witness and all I can think about is Prince lounging on an ornate purple stretcher, held by shirtless servants, like Cleopatra, that take him door to door to hand out those pamphlets that clog gutters. *Prince is too smart to walk that much in high heels.*

"Oh, absolutely." I say, "I totally believe in Jesus Christ *Superstar.* Can I save you? I forgot to ask you that when I first walked in the door. Thank you Jerome, for reminding me."

"You need to leave, Miss, and you know, *there's no way in Hades that you're 29!*"

I grab my white fur snow suit and bend over to place my foot into the first pant leg, preparing to leave. I hope *Not Jerome* is looking at my backside while I have time to come up with something. He's still frustrated by his crossword.

"Wait, wait, I don't want to leave yet. Being in Prince's entourage is on my bucket list of things to do before I turn *fifty*, I mean *thirty!* I'm even writing a book about it!"

"You, a writer?" Jerome asks, shaking his head.

I'm still perturbed about his "Hips lie" comment.

"Well, this new novel is going to be my breakthrough. I'll...I'll do anything to make it a success. Cleanse my naked body in the waters of Lake Minnetonka, if I have to. You'll just have to drive me there. I'm afraid I told my Underworld Uber driver to go."

"You're a dreamer and a fool," the man *so obviously Jerome* tells me.

"Yes, I dream a lot. Sometimes eight, nine dreams in a single night. Sometimes, I even have daydreams within my dreams. I'm brave in my dreams - a sexy, witty, problem solver like a seasoned MI6 Agent. I usually wake up in the morning melancholy and exhausted."

"I've heard enough, you're out of here! You could never be in Prince's entourage."

I spy the crossword for a quick second and thank the

Goddess for all my hours planted in front of the TV waiting for my father to return home after a long journey.

"Rhoda."

"What?"

"Spinoff of **The Mary Tyler Moore Show**? Thirty Across."

Jerome writes the word in.

"Fine, you're in," he reluctantly agrees.

I've just bought my ticket across!

It's more beautiful than I could've imagined, once I sail across those white beads. From afar, I hear my favorite lyrics of all, from **Little Red Corvette.**

I was weak, I tell you, weak in the knees, trying not to slide across the freshly polished floor in my stockings. I'm drenched in purple light and following what looks like the yellow brick road from **The Wizard of Oz,** and into a large Drawing Room with a dance floor, and mirrors on the walls. I'm instantly reminded of the **Kiss** video. *My nether regions sigh.*

At the end of the yellow brick road, there is a giant stage, with a golden throne. There he sits, in all his purple glory, Prince, in tight black pants and a purple paisley satin scarf around his neck, drinking Yoo-hoo, with his tiny feet dangling off the chair. A young acolyte dressed as a belly dancer stands beside him, holding a mirror. Prince turns his head toward the mirror to fix his hair every few minutes or so while he speaks.

"And you are?" Prince asks.

"Eddy E."

"Eddy E.?"

"Yes, like Sheila E. She's my cousin."

"What's your dance style?" Prince asks.

"Oh, you know, **Nasty Girl/Sex Shooter** living in an **Erotic City** looking for a **Love Bizarre**."

"Do you believe in God?" he asks. This line of questioning is getting old. I do not believe in God – *only Goddess!*

"Yes." I answer. "When I bought your album for the first time I thought I was looking at the face of Jesus. The older girls made me memorize and recite the lyrics to **Dirty Mind** at slumber parties, after threatening to put my hand in warm water while I slept so that I would pee on myself."

"I'm flattered and slightly nauseated at the same time, but

you didn't answer my question. Do you believe in God?"

I try to distract him with some sincere sucking up, "Only when I hear your music, Prince. Your songs, *the dirty ones.* "

I close my eyes and turn my face in shame for dramatic effect.

"The dirty ones? You know I stopped playing those in concert. I'm a man of God now."

"A man of God when you *wrote* those songs? Those lyrics, those melodies, well, they gave me...*tremors.*"

"I'm glad my music affected you so, Eddy E., but unfortunately, I can't play those songs anymore."

"That saddens me, Prince. I will never be able to take a bubble bath and not think of **The Ballad of Dorothy Parker**. And **It,** well, instead of singing, 'I want to do it all the time,' you should have just said, "I want to fuh- *forgive me, but you're just so confident about your sexuality. It's so much fun, living vicariously through you.* "

Prince smiles. I made Prince smile! I knew it – I'm AMAZING!

"But **Slow Love** and **Adore** can't be on that list. They're too beautiful. It would be a sin *not to play them*. I can understand

not playing **Head**, it sets up, well, and you know, *expectations for*

an evening? **Sometimes it Snows in April**? You and T.S. Eliot

are soulmates! I'm sorry the critics tore you a new one over your

film, **Under The Cherry Moon**. Damn fools! And, the song, **Sexy**

Mother Fucker? I'll get down on my knees this very moment and

thank Goddess for it. *Perfection!"*

    "Okay, okay, so you like my music," Prince says and lifts

his white gloved hands like Diane Wiest in **Bullets over**

Broadway. *Don't speak, don't speak.*

    "I think you're a musical genius."

    "Tell me, Eddy E. Why are you here?"

    "Oh, why am I here? Well, one of my items on my bucket

list before turning thirty is to be in your entourage."

    "Thirty?"

    "Yes, thirty. A few sit ups and a spray tan and I'm good to

go."

    Oh, shit! Prince is going to call me out on my shenanigans

any second now. It's not dark enough in this room to hide my

crows' feet.

"Well, you're not black."

"*But my soul is!* And you let Sheena Easton in and she's not black!"

"*Sheena can do the splits!*"

"Listen, Prince. If you want to see some titties wiggle and an ass shake, then I'm your girl!"

"Fine, but make it quick. I've got a mani/pedi in half an hour!"

First, Prince asks me to sing.

It was just like my **American Idol** audition all over again.

Prince contorts his face in pain at the sound of my voice and opens his mouth wide for some *lutefisk* hand fed to him by the young protégé fawning beside him. The patchouli incense burning throughout the room does nothing to diffuse the smell of the stinky fish.

In the purple light, Prince begins to look less like my idol, and more and more like Marlon Brando at the end of **Apocalypse Now**. He puts on black mascara in front of the hand held mirror while chewing loudly on the white gelatinous substance. It smells worse than Ash Wednesday in New Orleans. No wonder Paisley

Park has a fence around it.

Then, Prince asks me to dance.

But, I'm wearing fishnet stockings, and he just got the floors polished, and, well, I slip and fall onto my back, hitting my head. I hear my hair spray hair crunch against the wood and see stars until I realize it's just a disco ball hanging from the ceiling above me. I pull myself back up and onto my feet quickly, just like my personal trainer always tells me to. I need to demonstrate quick reflexes. I fear Prince might question my age again.

"*How white are you?*" he asks me, giggling. The Yoo-hoo Prince was just drinking shoots right out of his nose. "I need you to be exotic; Latin, bi-racial, a musician, a singer."

"I mean I *am* half Italian with a pinch of Greek. I can put a curse on your friend in the mud room, the one who's pretending he's *not Jerome*. I just need a goat and…and *a switchblade.*"

"Enough!" Prince is getting pissed. I'm wasting his time, and he needs another Yoo-hoo.

"*Jerome!*" Prince yells from his golden throne.

I knew it! I heard from the *Paisleyvine* Facebook Group, earlier that day, that Morris Day of The Time loaned Jerome out to

Prince in exchange for paying off some of his gambling debts to
the Minnesota Mob.

"Get this bitch out of here. She's CRAZY, *and she's old as*
hell! Get me another Yoo-hoo, dammit!"

Jerome strong arms me, finally dragging me by my feet as
my satin teddy slides across the shiny, sparkling dance floor.

"You'll regret this Prince!" I yell. "You suck Purple Ass!"
I scream mid-drag. "And so do the Vikings! I'm glad Warner
Brothers took your money!"

3 SLEEP WITH DAVID DUCHOVNY

When we meet at St. Mark's Bookshop in the Village,

Duchovny sits in a corner reading an **US Magazine** and eating

Kale soup.

"David." I begin, "I'm Eddy. Your agent told me I would

find you here."

"Hi, Eddy. Care for some soup?"

"No thanks."

"I'm a Pescatarian. It's a Vegetarian who eats fish."

"I think I figured it out, thanks."

Is Duchovny going to mansplain all day or drop his

drawers?

"So, Eddy, why are you here?"

"Well, I'm your biggest fan and I want to sleep with you before my birthday."

"Really? I'm flattered, but we just met. I hardly know you."

"Like that matters? I thought you were a nymphomaniac."

"Fine, you can *try* and give me a hand job," he says. "My anti-anxiety medication keeps me pretty limp though, F.Y.I."

"I'm the only person who actually *saw* your film, **House of D**, with Robin Williams as a second rate Rain Man, and all I get to do is give you a *hand job*?"

"I'm afraid I'm late for my two o'clock appointment; the life of a sex addict and all. You know, I'm booked for most of the day."

"I love you, David Duchovny. I thought you'd read me Irish poetry and then let me sit on your face."

"That's my four o'clock."

"Then, kiss me!"

"I only kiss women I love."

"Kundera? You're going to throw Milan Kundera in my

face? I know you were a Lit major at Princeton and all, but do you even know who I am? Do you have any idea who you're dealing with here?"

If we're going to have a literary battle, I want to dig my feet deep down into the trenches and get my fists up.

"You're nothing like the man I love. I hate you, DAVID DUCHOVNY!" I yell and grab my Agent Provocateur bag and Good Vibrations UPS box and start to head toward the door.

"I'm out of here you low brow, stinky Vegan!"

"Pescatarian!" he corrects.

"Whatever!" I yell back.

I grab the **US Magazine** out of his hands and hit him over the head with it. The sadist in me enjoys this. *I will spank his bare ass if necessary. Point me to the Red Room.*

"Ouch!" he says.

I throw the X-Files, Fox Mulder figurine I bought at Toys R Us at his head, and miss.

I throw an economy bottle of lubricant at his head that, at five pounds, could double as a hand weight for bicep curls. It makes contact with his beautiful face.

"Jesus, Eddy! That's gonna leave a mark," he says, covering his right eye with his hand. I picture him with an eye patch, like a pirate, and think, *yep, I'd still fuck him one-eyed.*

I throw the only thing left in my purse – a box of Magnum sized condoms. Overly ambitious, I know, *but that Internet video of him in a bathtub.*

"I'm smarter than you, David Duchovny, Mr. Ivy League, big-dick, New York bastard. And I just ate a burger 30 minutes ago – *rare!"*

I stick my tongue out for extra emphasis.

"You're a live wire, aren't you, Eddy?"

"I'm just a disappointed fan." I answer.

David Duchovny blocks the front door so I can't leave. He's taller than I am and his cashmere sweater smells like *Wild Alaskan Salmon and...warm chocolate chip cookies.*

"Wait, stay, and I'll cancel the rest of my afternoon for you," he insists.

"You will?"

"Just take me for a burger. The thought of red meat is getting my nipples hard. Then, I'll sleep with you, okay?"

"Oh, alright then."

We hold hands like sweethearts and take a taxi to Bryant Park on a quest for beef.

Sitting outside, beside the New York Public Library, surrounded by autumn leaves and Peeping Toms, Duchovny downs a double beef patty with bacon and French fries from Shake Shack. I sip on a chocolate shake, *which is my kind of foreplay.*

"The sex addict thing, it's just for publicity." he says, "It keeps me in the press. I really just visit my favorite store - *the GAP* - during those so called sex appointments."

"So, then, the well-endowed thing is also a gimmick *for the press?"* I ask.

"Oh no! Well, that actually *is* true. That's why I'm always at the GAP. *My life quest* is to find the perfect pair of pleated pants."

He licks the bacon grease off of his fingers, one by one. *I can think of something I'd like to lick.*

"I kind of don't like to talk about it – my size and all. It brings up *flashbacks*, you know?" Duchovny says.

"Flashbacks?" I ask.

23

"I…well, I nearly smothered a girl to death at a Club Med recently. She's pressing charges and we're trying to keep a lid on it. We're lucky because no one even knows what a Club Med is anymore."

I slam my hand down hard on the table, nearly breaking it.

"Wait! Stop! You mean to tell me that your dick is so big *that you nearly smothered a girl to death?"*

Duchovny just shrugs his shoulders.

"And we haven't met until now because…?" I demand, outraged.

"Well, I'm not allowed any funny business with women for the next nine months, or at least, that's what my lawyer tells me. I'm hopped up on anti-anxiety medication from the stress of it all. Couldn't get it up even if I wanted to. *Sorry."*

Duchovny wipes his extremely kissable mouth with a paper napkin and continues talking. "Thanks for the burger. I needed the iron. I'm practically anemic."

Goddam Vegans; I mean… *Pescatarians.*

"Hey, would you like to come over to my place and watch **Masterpiece Theater**? I have some gluten-free, vegan pot brownies in the freezer."

"I guess so."

Limp Dick Double D grabs my hand in his and flags a cab for us on Sixth Avenue.

We spend most of the night at his posh pad, reading aloud and laughing at his unfinished dissertation from Yale. I bribed his academic adviser months earlier to print me a copy. I practically knew it by heart; even the dated CBGB references.

"Let me guess, you've probably never been with more than a handful of men," Duchovny asks.

I hope he doesn't hear me swallow.

"Maybe less?" he tries again.

"You're wrong, David. I'm a big slut, and I've got the tramp stamp to prove it!"

I try to lift my shirt over my head to show David my lower back, but it's so tight that my arms get stuck.

"That's not a tattoo," he corrects.

"I'm sorry I lied to you. It's just a scar from a botched epidural."

"Sit here," he says and grabs my behind with both hands

and sits me on his lap. *Frisky*, I think, getting excited for a second, but then remember there's no chance we're hooking up tonight. Bummer. I'm wearing my best panties. I pull my shirt back down, embarrassed.

"Pick a book, any book, and I will read it to you."

Now this, *this gets me hot.* How did David know this is my biggest fantasy? *Best Boy, indeed.*

I grab **Franny and Zooey**, the less obvious choice, on his Salinger shelf, and sit back down on his warm lap.

"I heard you were the most well-read actor in Hollywood."

He reads me the whole book while we down two bottles of Chateau Margaux and eat the whole plate of brownies. Without the stress of a hard-on, I melt into Duchovny's arms and fall asleep. I never relax with men *or women for that matter.* I feel something open up inside of me for the first time in a long time. *Like, I could allow someone into my private world.*

Then, I hear Salinger's last words pertaining to the serenity of quiet sleep. Brownies finished and candles burned. I wake up to Duchovny gently kissing my forehead. God, he smells good – *like, like fresh Red Snapper.*

"I should go," I say as I turn my head trying to wipe the drool away from my chin without him noticing.

I gather my things but Duchovny remains sitting, looking up at me from his leather chair. I don't like it when men stare at me. It usually means they want to know the truth, or even worse, have me take my clothes off.

"It's a smokescreen, then?" David asks.

"What?"

I have a bad case of the munchies and will definitely be hitting a Bodega on the way home to pick up a ham and egg sandwich. Since there's no sex tonight, I'm stuffing my face.

"Your writing. I read your blog," he says.

"For reals?" I ask.

"Yes, I liked it. But, the language, the sexuality, it's all bullshit, isn't it? I can't even tell if you actually *like* sex. What are you hiding, Eddy? For reals?"

Goddam Genius he is, this David Duchovny. Just like Prince. No wonder he got a perfect score on his SAT Verbal. This is better than sex and I bet I can still get my money back from the 'Debauchery Box' with the *his and hers* vibrators I ordered from

San Francisco.

"I'd rather not talk about me. I'm super baked and the Psych 101 makes me paranoid."

"Still hiding." Mr. Know-It-All answers.

"You're smart, David Duchovny; not just a dick on a stick. You deserve your Ivy League pedigree. Now I know why I've always loved you. *You're smarter than the average bear.*"

"You're good at deflecting reality, aren't you? Why can't you tell me who you really are and what you really want. *You're safe here, Eddy.*"

"Please, *forget about me!* You're the celebrity." I say.

"Alright, then. Promise me, Eddy, that one day you will allow yourself to be vulnerable. *Let your waking life also be your fantasy world.*"

"I just want *to get under someone's skin.* Maybe that's why I'm a writer; it's safe."

"You want a connection?" David asks.

"Connection, yes!" I say, shrugging my shoulders and rolling my bloodshot brown eyes. Goddam Hollywood Hash. He's got me singing like Ethel Merman.

I make sure to put his Golden Globe trophy in my canvas *Books are Magic* bag before we leave his house at dawn. He'll forgive me for it later, I'm sure. It's a fair trade for the giant orgasm *I've* been robbed of.

David walks me, in flip flops and a pair of his signature Gap pleated pants, to the front of his brownstone to meet the Town Car he ordered for me.

"I'm glad we finally met," Duchovny says sweetly, smiling at me. I take a deep breath and notice how calm I am in his presence. *No candle needed. Or pills.* He's a giant lotus flower that I want to snack on all day. I just want to stay here, with him, but I know he's just a guide and one of many I will meet tonight.

"Me too, David. You're alright, you know that? You're not one of those *goddam phonies*. Why can't *you* be my best friend?"

"I can be, Eddy. There's more than one of me out there when you wake up, *I swear.* Trust me, *I've also studied the Greeks.* I know a great deal about this quest that you're on and I'm telling you to keep moving forward. *You've got this.*"

The car pulls up in front of us and the street is so quiet that all I hear is the engine running and the radio. I turn my head to listen to the song, **The World's A Mess; It's In My Kiss**. It's X – Duchovny's favorite band.

He leans over and kisses me square on the mouth with some force. Our tongue tips touching, *titillating*, which only makes me mourn his temporary impotence even more.

"You broke your rule!" I yell.

"That burger is dangerous."

Goddam *Know-It-All* men with New York accents. Goddam Salinger.

And then I climb into the car, close the door and roll down the window.

"Do you want to see *it*?" he asks coyly.

"*It*?" I ask.

"*Me*?"

He looks down, below his belt and then back up into my eyes.

"Um…*yes…abso-fucking-lutely!*"

Duchovny leans over and kisses me again. He unbuttons the top button of his pants and slowly pulls down his zipper. My mouth starts watering, but I blame the THC. *I'm so happy right now.*

"*Gotcha!*" he says and smiles at me while pulling the zipper back up and buttoning the top of his pants. He waves goodbye and walks back toward the brownstone laughing. I'm also laughing at his right eye shiner now revealed in the soft sunlight, the price of a heavy and sadly unused bottle of lube thrown at his face some hours earlier.

"Goodnight, Eddy!" the person I wish was my best friend yells.

"Goodnight, Asshole!" I yell back, out the car window, as we turn onto First Ave and I anticipate my breakfast sandwich.

4 BE IN A SORORITY

It never occurred to me to try and be in a sorority. Freshman year of college, my roommate belonged to a religious cult and a family of industrial spies.

She was rushing and asked if I wanted to. I didn't want to spend any more time with her than I had to. I said I wasn't sure.

Then, I shared a smoke with the skinny Mormon ROTC girl on our floor who told me that rushing was "bad news." She'd been to a party the previous night where someone asked her *what her father did for a living*.

"Pool Hustler," I'd answer. The room would fall silent and then I'd quickly be escorted out the door; or so I thought, back then.

It always seemed like the sorority girls had it all, so when rush came this year, I wasn't going to be missing out. I was going to be accepted into one of these houses and finally wear the letters I deserved!

The first house I try is the Jewish one. I think it's a piece of *noodle kugel,* with letters sent on my behalf, from a boy I used to like in grammar school, who had spent a summer at a Kibbutz.

"So, I'm not familiar with the initiation process, but it can't be any worse than what my Uncle Short had to do to get into the Chicago 'Outfit' is it?"

"It's not happening," a girl named Sandy tells me, over high tea in the house living room. I'd kill for her shoes.

"Why not?" I plead.

"You're not Jewish."

"But, I've been raised in the Jewish community. My godmother is Jewish and I even went to Temple as a child."

"Sorry." Sandy tells me.

"So going to nearly thirty Bar and Bat Mitzvahs in the years 1983-86 doesn't count for anything!?" I yell back, slamming the door behind me.

The second house I show up at is for Southern Belles.

"Wow! This house is really pretty," I tell the Sorority President, Sally. "I've never seen so much...*toile.*"

"Thank you. We like old and classic here."

"That's a good thing because my family is very old and prominent. I'm a DAR and my mother has Jamestown descendants on both sides."

"Yes, we looked you up and you do have that, on the one side, but at the end of the day, your people who crossed the Atlantic were indentured servants and are now MAGA hat-wearing Hillbillies."

"I'm offended!"

"And, well, I won't even begin to go into your father's side."

"What about my father's side?"

"More Hillbillies."

The Third Sorority I show up at is the African-American one. They're confused when I arrive.

"You *do* realize this is a black sorority, don't you?" the President, Janice tells me.

"Um, of course I do. I was hoping you could teach me how

to dance if I live here? I might still have a shot of getting into Prince's entourage."

"Are you even are a student here?" Janice asks, losing patience with me.

"Um, next question?"

"You're insulting me AND you're old enough to be my mother. We would never take you," Janice tells me.

"I'm sorry, I'm sorry! *I'm desperate.* My birthday is tomorrow and I've never been in a sorority. It's on my list of regrets."

"Alright, well, why don't you try the house next door?"

The girls standing behind Janice whisper and laugh in unison, and I stand up and leave.

The fourth and final sorority I end up at is the Zeta Theta...*whatever*. It's the *zaftig thumb sucker house.* This is embarrassing, *even for me.*

I open the door to find a bunch of fat girls in glasses eating bowls of potato chips, drinking *regular* Coke and watching *The Mandalorian.* For Christ Sake, *Baby Yoda won't get you laid!*

"Ever hear of an eating disorder? Its time you all got one,"

I say.

"What do you want?" asks Betts, the Sorority President, who stands up in Hello Kitty pajamas to address me, meekly.

"Ladies, today is your lucky day. I'm here to help you, and at the same time, help myself, because I'm nothing if not a megalomaniac." I begin, "Let's face facts. First of all, you're all losers."

A few of the girls begin to cry. One takes out her retainer because she's choking on her own saliva.

"But you don't have to stay that way!"

"So, what do you intend on doing?" Asks Puffy, soon to be my new bestie.

"I'm going to make you popular. I might be another year older tomorrow, but I still have my reputation to consider. My Facebook friends pay very close attention to organizations I like."

"Facebook?" Betts asks, "Damn, you are old!"

"What do we need to do?" Puffy asks.

"You only need two things to be popular in college. First – let everyone think you're easy. Second - *let everyone think you have the best drugs.*"

My *Sisters* all look at each other in amazement. *This isn't brain surgery girls; it's college.*

"Let's start with the best drugs. Tell me - which house on campus has the most guys from New Jersey?"

We get to Jersey House and knock on the door. A stoned twenty-year-old named Stu opens and then slams the door right in my face. "Your Mom is here man, hide everything! And she's with one of those fat girls."

I knock on the door a second time, pissed.

"I'm not old enough to be your Mother! I need to talk to you. I need some shit, the good stuff!"

"Hold it down." Stu pleads with me as he opens the door, "Come in."

I step over empty Popeye's and Domino's boxes and a few toilet paper rolls to get to a room with a television and stereo that only Michael Bloomberg could afford.

"Wow! Impressive!" I say to Tony, the big man in charge who sits in a brown, tweed Lazy Boy recliner covered in cigarette burn holes. "What's good?" I ask.

"Oh, you know…" Tony says.

"Actually, I don't know. I don't do drugs, never have. But all of my friends do, well, I *mean did.* Bring whatever's hot; Ecstasy, Blow, I don't care. Bring it to the Zeta Theta, *wait, what's it called?"*

"Zeta Theta Psi," Puffy says.

"Bring it to the house on Friday night. We're having a Party," I say.

"Really? Those girls don't have parties."

"Well, now they do. Puffy, give this guy your Rolex as a down payment."

Puffy hands her Rolex over to Tony reluctantly and starts to walk out the door.

"Puffy, meet me in the car," I say.

"Biggest sluts you've ever met, *those girls,*" I tell Tony and Stu and anyone else conscious enough to listen. "Like a turnstile their front door. And Puffy, the one you just met, *I heard she went down on a girl once."*

We're on our third showing of Jillian Michael's exercise DVD in the living room of my new Sorority House, when *she* walks in, the girl destined to ruin my life.

"Penny!" Puffy yells, trying to get out of doing the next set of lunges.

"How was your night with Chase?" Puffy asks.

Penny, goddam Doppelganger she was. Hair, ass, tits - *All Big.* She had exactly thirty pounds on me and nails bitten down, bloody and raw. Did this quest have to include a reminder of who I *used to be*?

"It was… *interesting*," Penny whispers.

The way Penny blushes, averting her eyes, hunching her shoulders to hide her chest. I know that look. She's a virgin. Fuck me.

"*I think I brown balled him,*" Penny continues.

Yep, virgin.

"For the record," I begin, "the term is *blue balled*, and that's a good thing. All of you ladies, listen up! Blue balling? GOOD! *Indiscriminate cock sucking? BAD!* You should always make a man suffer before he gets to have you; it's the only way to keep him and the only way he'll respect you. But don't listen to me, I'm only in my *mid to late thirties.*"

I think they buy it.

"Really?" Penny asks. It's hard to look at her face, it's so familiar. She even smells like a virgin, like Caddy from William Faulkner's **Sound and The Fury**!

"They might *claim* they'll die from blue balls, *but its total bullshit.*" It's important to pass this information down a generation. *You're welcome, Gloria Steinem.*

"Then, I'm doing the right thing?" Penny asks. *Goddess, she has perky tits. Does she even need to wear a bra?*

"How long have you known this guy? You like just met him, right?" I ask.

"No, actually. We've been friends for a while - studied together. He just started getting interested in me all of a sudden. Jumped me a few weeks ago. I never thought he thought of *me like that*, you know, *like a girlfriend.*" Penny says, trying to sort it all out.

"*Girlfriend?* Okay, let's not get ahead of ourselves here. You've been with other guys, right?"

"No, I mean he's my first. Although we've never…"

"He's super popular then, a Fraternity guy?"

"No, actually, he's one of those fringe, arty guys. Makes

me laugh – a lot. He's a DJ," Penny says with a smile.

"But he plays really bad music, right? Like Milli Vanilli, *without irony?"*

There has to be something wrong with this guy.

"I don't know who Milli Vanilli is, but no, not them. Really cool, old time bands like The Kinks and the poet Leonard Cohen."

"Of, course. *He chooses the soundtracks for Wes Anderson movies, too, I bet?"* I say, increasingly more annoyed.

"But he's kind of...*weird?"* Penny says, intriguing me.

"Listen to me, the weird arty guy in college ends up being a huge success later in life!"

"Really? I do like that he's so odd."

Now I know Penny is a pervert. Goddess, what is the point of all of this?

"Even nail biting zaftig girls can become supermodels one day," I try and assure her.

"Were you a super model?" Penny asks.

"No, but I lost thirty pounds. You will, too. Work with me here."

"He's from New York."

Of course, he is. That's it. I can't take any more of this flashback. If I look into Medusa's face one more time, I'll turn into stone!

"Puffy, get me a White Claw and the bottle of Xanax from my purse. And turn off that incessant Jillian Michaels on the TV! I need to lay down."

I pass out on the sofa.

I wake up an hour later with Penny staring down into my face. She smells like Honeysuckle and all things pure, just the way I used to smell once.

"What was that?" Penny asks.

"A panic attack. Like *you've* never seen one before?"

"No."

Okay, maybe she isn't necessarily my Doppelganger. Just Persephone out of Hades for a quickie with her lover?

"Okay, which one of you girls has the biggest bedroom?" I ask.

Puffy raises her hand.

"Okay, I'll be sleeping in your room tonight. The rest of you, take it easy. Enjoy *being young, dumb girls.*"

I climb into Puffy's Princess bed and look up at a Post Malone poster. *Face tattoos are baller.* I call my mother on the red landline that looks exactly like the one we had in our kitchen growing up. I've missed hearing her voice. In this alternate reality, I have access to anyone I want, dead or alive. It makes me feel powerful. I regret driving my parent's nuts with desperate calls pleading for their help while at college. I was so scared of growing up. I held on to them too tightly.

"Why was I such a loser, mother?" I ask.

"We don't call it loser, remember, honey? We call it *late bloomer.*"

"Seriously, why wasn't I more confident in my youth? Why didn't you send me to Fat Camp or something? I blame you for all of this, you know."

"Your therapy made my insurance premiums skyrocket. I don't want to hear any more about it. And I'm sure *your children would like to talk to you.* You're going to have to wake up sometime, Eddy."

"Not now, mother, I'm too depressed."

"You're not even fifty yet. Wait till your actual birthday.

Then, you'll be depressed."

"As always, you've cheered me up, Mother. Slitting my wrists now. Goodnight."

I hang up the phone and fall asleep quickly from the Xanax. I dream of eating a hoagie on the Jersey Shore with Jillian Michaels.

Next morning, revitalized and ready for retail therapy, I announce, "Okay, if you've got a black American Express card, please follow me."

Three girls step forward.

"We're going shopping."

Later, that night, in Puffy's bedroom, I help her try on the new, couture outfits for the party, and wax her mustache. Puffy hangs up the phone.

"Hermes is saying 4-6 weeks for delivery of your Birkin bag."

"Oh good." I say.

Penny walks in. I'd avoided her all day.

"Well, we *almost* did it tonight. He kept asking me if he should put a condom on and I didn't answer."

I have to be a responsible adult now. I thought I was *escaping reality!*

"So, Penny, *do you want to fuck...*"

I correct myself quickly, *language.*

"I mean...*make love* to him, *this...*" I continue.

"Chase," Penny answers.

"Chase," I confirm. "Cute name as well," I add.

"I think I do."

"Well, you realize you might just be friends, right?" I say, from the bottom of my heart. I'm in love with this Penny and don't want her to get hurt like I did, decades before.

"He told me he loved me. He said I was *beautiful,*" Penny says modestly.

"Puffy, get me another cocktail and my pills, please." I order.

Instead of letting this be Penny's moment, I start sobbing. Puffy fears I'll black out again.

"What is it; what's wrong?" Penny asks.

"Nothing's wrong, Penny. I'm just so happy for you. He told you...*you were beautiful?*"

"Your first, *did he tell you that?"*

"*Not exactly*. I'd be a different person today if he had, Penny."

"Do you ever think about it? Your first time?" Penny asks. *Goddess, doesn't this girl have a mother of her own?*

"I try not to."

"Really?" Penny looks at me, worried.

"No, I'm just kidding. *Puffy, where's that drink?"*

"I'd like you to meet Chase," Penny says, excited.

"Why?" I ask. I shouldn't have anything to do with this girl, or her... *deflowering.*

"I want your *okay,"* Penny says. She feels a connection to me. I wish she didn't.

"Sure, I'll meet him, but it's *your decision*. And if everything you've told me is true, he sounds like a good one. *Just wear a condom, okay?"*

My parenting advice – finished for the night.

"Now, please leave me alone. I'm just so happy for you Penny. I've been known to punch people in the face when I'm this Happy," I say as I shoo her away.

Puffy returns with a La Croix vodka and some pills. I take

a sip of the drink and spit it out.

"Dammit, Puffy, *can't you do anything right?"*

It's the big day – the day of the party – and I'm hopeful. I

want my Sorority sisters to have fun. I get them, truly I do, and

they deserve some positive attention. Every young girl does.

They look so gorgeous. Surprise! Expensive clothes, the

right amount of cleavage and an aesthetician can do a lot for a girl.

The Jersey guys come early to make a delivery of Molly

and drink all the best booze. Sloppy Stu hits on girls who

quickly shut him down.

Chase shows up and both his and Penny's eyes dilate when

they catch each other across the crowded living room. I can't

watch them for much longer because their young love is as

nauseating as Prince's lutefisk.

The girls start *Chase the DJ's* Spotify playlist and the songs

are incredible, with just the right mix of Glam Rock and New

Wave for my fragile, Gen X heart. Is there anything Chase doesn't

do perfectly?

Penny barely speaks when Chase approaches her. He does

most of the talking and Penny hides her face behind her big head

of hair. She's nervous. Although Chase is witty arty boy, I can tell

he's nervous as well. Now that they've seen one another naked, he's

a little self-conscious.

Stu randomly talks to anyone who will listen. His eyes

look like saucers.

"Move your ass!" he yells at Penny, our Penny, the girl

loved by both Chase and me. The girl I always wanted to be.

Penny's giant smile turns into a frown and it's as though the

driver of her carriage has turned back into a mouse.

I retract my arm, thanking Jillian Michaels for my taut

bicep, and prepare to clock this scumbag Stu to high heaven, but I

get there too late.

It's Chase. He gets there first, and now Stu, the composite

of every single asshole I ever crossed paths with at college, lays

flat on the floor from a perfectly executed punch.

Chase and Penny are shocked by the electricity of their

adrenaline rush. They look at each other and know that they, in

fact, *connect.*

Penny turns her head toward me to see the message I'm

sending her. He's... the one...and it's going to happen...*tonight*!

"This is Chase," she tells me, as she grabs my hand and pulls me toward him.

"Hi there, handsome," I say to Chase. "You're quite the hero tonight." *Like a young Paris,* I think.

"He's my hero." Penny states, looking down, still just an observer in her own, new to feeling attractive, girl world. *You're my hero, Penny.*

"We should go," Chase says.

"Sure, just let me get my coat," Penny answers.

Chase and I are left alone. I want to say the right thing, the best thing for Penny, the best thing for both Penny and Chase.

"I hope wherever life takes you, Chase, that you never forget this girl. She's amazing."

"Penny's not like other girls. I don't think I could ever forget her."

"Well, promise me you won't block her from your Instagram page, 30 years from now," I say.

"I promise," Chase snickers.

Penny returns with her coat and the couple leave the house

hand in hand.

I spend the rest of the night holding straightened hair back while some of the girls hurl. I'm happy to say a few engaged in some minor petting, and a few gave their numbers out. Puffy and Betts are planning the next party. Mission accomplished! Eddy's Home Makeover: Sorority Edition complete!

Early the next morning, I'm cleaning in an OCD fit, making breakfast and coffee for all the girls. I do like being a mother. *I wonder how my kids are doing.* Penny walks in wearing her clothes from the night before. Her long brown hair is damp and smells like Easter lilies from the Lincoln Park Conservatory I visited with my mother as a child.

"Come here, sweetheart," I tell her.

"I'm pretty exhausted from last night," Penny tells me and her Sorority sisters. "But..."

"You can't stop smiling?" I say.

"Yeah."

Penny - innocent, sweet girl, without any makeup on, gives me a half-smile for the photo I snap from my phone. I want to remember my *much happier than I was, deflowered Doppelganger.*

Mimosas for everyone!

"Here, eat some eggs," I tell her and put a plate in front of her and pour some Prosecco into her orange juice.

"Actually, it wasn't too bad," she says, swirling the yellow food with her fork on the plate, face glowing. "It was nice, actually." If only I could scrape the pixie dust off of her and bottle it.

Mr. Perfect Chase, is just that – *Perfect.*

I feel at peace about Penny. I feel at peace about myself and my own first time. I'm relieved to know that I've managed to wipe another slate clean.

"Thank you for helping me move forward dear girl, but my work here is done," I say, grabbing my new Hermes bag. *Things happen fast in alternate realities.*

"Wait, Wait!" Puffy says, "We have a shirt - *with letters on it, for you."*

I look at the shirt. It's a thin, pink, crop top with the Sorority letters - *whatever the hell they are. I don't know Greek – but tonight, I might learn.*

"It's beautiful," I say, "but I know the rules. You can't

wear letters unless you're *actually in a sorority.* It was super fun pretending though."

I walk out of the door and away from the house, away from the girls, away from my Artemis twin, Penny, and instantly propel forward into my next adventure.

5 BE A TORCH SINGER

The first time I heard Chan Marshall's voice was on a Cat Power song, and we clicked instantly. It was 1995 and I found her on a mix tape sent from overseas. Separated at birth, we were; Chan Marshall and I, *convinced*; an "AHA!" moment. My long lost twin showing up during Soap Opera Sweeps Week. Although the cassette would eventually suffer death by meat tenderizer, it was too late, the bond had been made, our destiny had been set. She was my other half, this "Chan Marshall" and the torch singer that I always wanted to be.

"This is music people commit suicide to," my roommate said, after hearing Cat Power a few too many times. "It's like blow your brains out, stick your head in an oven."

"I know, don't you love it? It's just so visceral, *so real!"*

"Why do you love it so much?" my roommate asked. "Why do you love *her* so much? I mean, I get it, its intense, it can be *darkly romantic.* It's about love, *like, not having any?"*

"She's a torch singer," I say, "and I was born to be a torch singer. Plus, we share the SAME BIRTHDAY!"

"You want to be in a constant state of unrequited love, don't you?"

"All great artists are."

"Well, if you play her in the house one more time, I'm going to blow *your* brains out." She continued, "It's not, you know, *healthy* for you to listen to this all day long."

"What do you mean?"

"You're...*impressionable*...and kind of *volatile*."

I knew what she was referring to, random spurts of anger and violence resulting in the destruction of my vintage bedroom set. Cat Power had nothing to do with it. In fact, it was Yo La Tengo's album, **Painful,** that was the real culprit. Goddam Ira, Georgia and James and their melancholy melodies.

"She's nuts," my friend finished, having made her case.

"A temperamental artist," I argued. "Hey, aren't you the

same girl who put the theme song to **Midnight Cowboy**,

Everybody's Talkin' on our answering machine? Now that

song, *that's depressing!* The last thing I want is a dream with

Ratso Rizzo in it."

"Fine, play Cat Power all you want, just wear headphones!"

She screamed; her time of the month, *sure of it.*

Chan Marshall sang like Billie Holiday and Janis Joplin,

you know, "damaged?" The first time I saw Cat Power live, her

back faced the crowd like an esoteric Thelonious Monk and she

crooned like a certifiable crazy person. After yelling at the

audience to be quiet, she ran off the stage, and into a hallway near

the coat check. She turned every handle of every door in that hall

until she found one unlocked. I watched all of this and we made

eye contact briefly. I saw myself in that half second.

Chan slammed the door behind her and I heard her sobbing

in the restroom. I placed my hand up on the old Oak door, *gently*,

in an effort to connect with her. Twins are often lost without the

other - *or so I'd heard.* I wanted to tell her, "You don't have

to come out if you don't want to."

So, I'm standing in an alley outside of Schuba's bar waiting for the bus boy to take out the garbage at around 9pm. At my age, I'd accumulated what I thought was enough damage to sing a torch song properly.

I sneak into Chan Marshall's dressing room thinking that I'm a few steps ahead of the game. Like a CIA Field Agent, I have electrical tape to tape her to a chair, a bandana to gag her and a bottle of Bourbon for me to assuage my guilt. I merely planned on incapacitating her for *one* song - then, I would set her free. We would drink Bourbon together and braid each other's hair. She was going to be my best friend. *Twins always are.*

I wanted to sing one song, you know? Before my birthday? Even Woody Allen let Diane Keaton sing **It Seems Like Old Times** in **Annie Hall**. That was brave. I wanted to be brave like her, like Annie Hall.

I was surprised at what I saw in the dressing room when I turned the lights on. There were three computer screens showing stock market links, a Tucker Carlson poster on the wall, a macramé blanket over the chair with "Nixon 72'" embroidered on it and a half-drunk Kombucha on the desk. I wanted us to be alike;

she would know all of my deep dark secrets and desires, *wouldn't she?*

WHAMMO! I'm hit hard on the neck and knocked unconscious.

I wake up in the chair under the Nixon blanket; *my* body tied down with electrical tape and the bandana around *my* mouth. I look across the room to see Chan Marshall reading the stock tape on MSNBC and eating Greek Yogurt. It was like discovering a peanut M 'n' M stuck in a car seat, while battling PMS. I was *that* happy! I think, *"My long lost twin. Finally, we meet!"*

She notices that my eyes are open and puts the yogurt down. I see her typing on a keyboard and wearing a *navy Ann Taylor pantsuit. Huh?*

She barks into her phone, "Yeah, buy Big Blue, William Buffet just did! He's a closet liberal, but we'll take his economic lead. I just wired you the funds." She turns the phone off and turns up the volume on Fox News. I hope she's not doing it to cover my screams while she dismembers me.

"Think you'd get one over on the old Chanster, did you?"

Chanster?

"I studied with the Mossad in Israel. Don't worry about the loud music, I could have killed you an hour ago, but I don't have time to chop you up and bleach the floor before the show starts. Plus, I just bought these Clark's Easy Spirit loafers on Black Friday. God, I love Capitalism!"

I couldn't decide what freaked me out more - the fact that Chan Marshall jokes about almost killing me or the fact that she wears Easy Spirits?

"Alright, I'm going to take the bandana off and you're going to tell me why you broke into my dressing room."

She pulls out a shotgun from under her desk and points it at me.

"Just no screaming, okay?"

Once the bandana comes off, I take a deep breath.

"You're not one of those crunchy, liberal, lesbian stalkers?"

"No, I'm your twin and one of your biggest fans."

"What do you mean, *twin*?"

"We have the same birthday."

"We do? So that's the only reason you're here? Not to rip my Ann Taylor pantsuit off and make sweet lesbian love to me, but to wish me a Happy Birthday?"

"Yes, that's it! Although, 'sweet lesbian love' *is* on my list of things I've not done before. I'm game if you are?"

"Well, then?"

"Oh, you want to know why I'm here? Well, I want to be a torch singer. I want to sing a gut wrenching, sad song on stage, before my birthday."

"Not exactly the worst request," she says, putting the shotgun down to chug a bottle of Immodium.

"I have stage fright and it gives me ulcers," Chan says. "That's why I have to drink all this junk and eat the yogurt."

"Oh, I'm so sorry. I have stage fright, too. Not usually in front of a crowd, but one on one - *definitely.* If I'm alone with one person, a man usually, I get restless. I'm afraid of, *you know, having to be myself?"*

"To be an artist, you have to reveal yourself. It's an essential part of creating. It should come from a place that no one has seen yet."

"Well, the way you make it sound, it's beautiful, and not so scary."

She sits down in a chair and looks at me.

"In my spare time, I'm a Tea Bagger," she says.

"You like balls in your mouth?" I ask, confused. *Everything about this night is confusing.*

"No!" she answers.

"You can't possibly mean...?" I ask.

"I'm a Republican," she says. "Libs are all lizard, baby eating, Commie scum."

Oh, no, I feel a Qanon conspiracy coming on. I'd love a sip of that Bourbon now.

"You need to educate yourself, watch Fox News," she continues.

She puts a bright red MAGA hat on my head.

"If you play my latest album backwards, you will hear Newt Gingrich's first Congressional acceptance speech," she finishes.

"Right," I say, shaking my head. *What have I gotten into? I'm a naïve fool and this Siren is showing her true, hideous form.*

"What do you do, other than stalk card carrying, NRA members who Tik Tok with Rand Paul, and are also great torch singers?"

"I'm a writer."

"Really? What have you written?"

"Movies, TV pilots, short stories, a novel. But I haven't made a dime from any of it. I wouldn't mind an Ann Coulter pay day."

"Ann Coulter? *Baller!* " Chan chuckles, "My life regret – not doing a duet with Lil' Troy."

"No shit!"

I'm thinking more Cypress Hill, **Insane in the Brain**

"What do you write?"

"Oh, you know, *the lovable loser?* The girl who's always one step away from getting everything she wants. She can't figure out what she's doing wrong, *but the audience knows."*

"And what's she doing wrong?"

"Everything."

"Now, I just feel sorry for you. If we're twins, then why don't we have more in common? You're a physically weak Libtard who suffers from delusions of grandeur. If I were you, I would also be sad about your birthday."

"Thanks...*Sis.*"

"Why not create a persona for yourself like I did?"

"I've probably created *too many personas.* No one knows me."

"Look at me - ladies' lunches with Kimberly Guilfoyle by day - tortured Cat Power persona by night. My politics, my private life, *it stays private.*"

"I guess that makes sense," I answer. *"*My private life might stay a little too private. I'd like to share it with someone, sometime...you know?"

Being taped into a chair and forced to speak is definitely an enhanced interrogation technique. Can Cat Power mention this new tool to my therapist?

"You should've saved your money, like me. I'm not planning on singing forever. I have a plan. I'm actually a Certified Financial Planner and I'm managing a 200 million dollar hedge fund right now. After *my* big birthday, I'm buying Greek stocks on the cheap and retiring."

"There's a definite Greek theme here tonight."

"*That's what she said,*" Chan says and winks at me.

Not a lesson I want to learn tonight, Chan. I need to get out of this chair.

"Please, please, let me sing! I've already been turned down once!" I beg.

"Who turned you down?"

"Oh, *nobody special.*" I hope Prince and Chan aren't friends.

"Alright, I give up. Let me hear you."

I get to sing! I clear my throat.

I start to sing, **"Love Me or Leave Me"** and come to terms that *David Sedaris's Billy Holiday impression is definitely better than mine.*

"Stop!" Chan yells, "God that was awful." Chan shakes her head. "Perhaps murdering you would have been the smarter thing."

"No, no, no!" I say, "One more chance. It's hard to get air into my diaphragm tied up like this."

"Fine, but hurry it up, I need to change soon. *Gotta give the pinkos what they're paying for - earthy hipster: barefoot and braless.*"

"Velvet Underground." I say, **"Found a Reason."**

Chan allows me to sing a few verses this time and wipes my eyes with a tissue, shotgun between her legs.

"Now that's what I'm talking about. That's real, that's *you*!" she says. "Can't be a great torch singer without pain or a longing for something."

I suddenly realize, *that's the old me.* I start to smile.

This time, Chan's confused.

"What's your name?" she asks.

"Eddy," I answer.

"Listen, Eddy, maybe we are twins," Chan Marshall aka Cat Power says. "Without a longing in our hearts, there would be no art."

"I guess I was damaged."

"All great artists are." Chan shakes her head.

"But I'm not anymore," I answer. "Hooray!" I'd pump my fists in the air if my hands weren't taped behind my back. "Maybe being so depressed when I was younger was just a distraction, *a persona.* A way to avoid being present – *and grateful."*

"You're getting far too sentimental for me now, Eddy. Ayn

Rand is rolling in her grave."

She begins to remove the tape from the chair.

"How about I sing a song *for you* on stage? What would you like to hear?"

"The Greatest," I answer. "I can't think of a better torch song to hear on the eve of one's birthday."

"Wow! I can't believe we'll both be celebrating our birthdays on the same day – *January 21st.*"

I'm almost completely free from the chair.

"*The 20th, I thought?* You, me and David Lynch? The greatest artists of the twentieth and twenty-first centuries?"

"NO! My birthday is on the 21st!" she yells in my face with crazy back in her eyes. She lifts her fists up again and I brace for the blow.

"But we're both Aquarians!" I scream, my last words, before being knocked out.

I wake up beside a dumpster behind Burrito's As Big As Your Head.

"Ouch!" I say, brain throbbing into my skull.

Krav Maga must be *hella* magic, because all of a sudden, I

remember that *I don't need torch songs anymore.* Haven't listened to them in years. Although beautiful and seductive at first, they kept me stuck in the same place; sinking, slowly drowning in my own tears. I've sailed *so far* from this moment in time. Is that the point of this lesson? That I've changed? That I used to think one way about myself and *now I don't think that way anymore?*

HOLY SHIT - I AM CAPABLE OF CHANGE! *Ahoy, Matey!*

6 HAVE A STEPPERS' PARTY

The south side of Chicago is where great music is made. Muddy Waters, Howlin' Wolf and Etta James recorded there. House Music was invented there. Most importantly, "Steppers' Parties" take place there.

I grew up on the north side of Chicago, which might have something to do with the fact that I am *not* that great of a dancer. My cousins all live on the south side of Chicago and are the best dancers I know.

Weddings are obscenely large and extravagant family affairs where my relatives dance all night. The DJ is deliberated before the girl even gets a ring. Even my eighty-year-old Great Aunt gets out of her wheelchair to do the **Electric Boogie**. I may not own a floor length chinchilla that has fallen off a truck to barter with, but I would give up my college education to be able to dance as well as they do. Every time I try and join them on the dance floor at a baptism or a graduation, I quickly lose the beat and I hear them whisper to themselves, *"It's not her fault, she grew up on the north side."*

Well, I've decided that before my birthday, this is all going to change. I'm going to throw a traditional, south side of Chicago "Steppers' Party" for my birthday. I love "Steppers' Parties" because you can be eight-years-old or eighty and still participate. It's an innocent affair and not overtly sexual. A man and woman get dressed in their finery and come together on the dance floor, getting to know one another better. I find this to be sweet, and, even though Cat Power called me a lizard, I still have an ounce or two of warm blooded romanticism in me.

Now, all I have to do is break R. Kelly, the singer of the song, **Step In the Name of Love** and from the South Side of Chicago, out of jail to host it. Shouldn't be a problem - *things happen fast in alternate realities.*

_____

It's easy getting to R. Kelly's house. He lives on a block

wedged between President Obama and Minister Louis
Farrakhan, so it's on a tourist map. I also talked my way onto a
Junior High School bus, *which used to make* stops at R. Kelly's.

I jump off the bus with a bag of hot "Ribs N' Bibs" BBQ in
one hand. Everyone knows it's the best BBQ in the area, and a way
I can pay tribute to the south side roots Kelly and I share. I walk up
to the gate to find it unlocked and push it open and walk into the
house. With the Secret Service and the Muslim Brotherhood
watching the block with semi-automatic weapons, R. Kelly can
skimp on security.

I make my way through the giant rooms of the old mansion
until I find a room with a stage, spotlight, and throne for Mr. Kelly
– just like Prince! I hear **Step in the Name of Love** in the
distance. *There's a Steppers' party going on and I'm going to
dance!* As soon as I walk into the ballroom, the music stops and R.
Kelly contorts his face and asks, "Who the hell are you?"

"Hi R!" I yell.

R just looks at me, puzzled.

"You don't mind if I call you R, do you? I'm a really big
fan. I've forgotten all about the Golden Shower video a few years

ago. In an alternate reality, *it wasn't you."*

"It wasn't me," R says.

"You, Woody Allen and Roman Polanski are the worst. You made me love your work before I found out you were child molesters."

"Alleged."

"Listen R, I brought you some Ribs N' Bibs and was wondering if, in return, you could throw me an old fashioned South Side Steppers' party for my birthday? It's the only way I can earn the respect of my cousins who all live on the South Side and think I'm an uptight...*dork."*

"I don't do white girl steppers' parties! It's a black excellence thing, got it?"

"If it makes you feel any better, my own father told me 'white people stole everything from the blacks and made it shit.' He learned how to play pool at 63rd and Cottage Grove."

"Damn straight."

"Listen, you and I, well, we have a connection. We take great risks with our art, sometimes to the point of, well, *humiliating ourselves.* When you wrote **(Trapped) In the Closet,**

I just thought, *man, I get it, if nobody else does.*"

"You do? You get **(Trapped) In the Closet**?"

"Um, hello! Like *lived* it!"

"I appreciate your appreciation for black music and culture, but a steppers' party is strictly a black thing. I can't condone this."

"But I dream about this party. You and Ne-Yo are there, and you've written a Steppers' song just for me!"

"Somebody talking about me?" says a soothing voice from behind a curtain.

"Ne-Yo. No way! I love your many hats. You're so dapper!"

"Come Closer." Ne-Yo sings.

"Yes!"

"What do you want?" Ne-Yo asks.

"A Steppers' party for my birthday. Please!"

"I don't think that's such a big deal, I love Chicago girls."

"Thank you SO much. You have no idea how happy I am to hear this!"

"Fine!" R reluctantly agrees, "I just made parole, don't

make me regret this!"

"You know R, your song, **Happy People**, always cheers me up when I'm blue. And **Bump n' Grind.** I like…*the idea of it.* The older I get, *I don't see nothing wrong either!"*

"Thanks for your support," R. Kelly answers. "My fee is two million dollars."

"Two million dollars! Um, can we work out *a payment plan?"*

"This ain't Sallie Mae - *Hell no!"*

R walks off the stage, annoyed.

"Well, I guess it was a pipe dream, *the 'Steppers' party.'* I'll just curl up in bed with a bottle of Bourbon. Happy birthday to me!" I say, starting to head out the door.

"How about we have a little *private Steppers' party* right now?" Ne-Yo asks.

Ne-Yo is such a girl-lover, a gentleman, just like his videos.

DJ Casper's **Cha Cha Slide** starts to play. *Ne-Yo and I are going to step together? Hell yes!*

R comes out from behind the stage curtain, furious.

"Damn you, Ne-Yo! You know I can't resist this song!"

I'm doing the **Cha Cha Slide** with Ne-Yo and R. Kelly? Will anyone ever believe me?

I hear clapping from behind the curtain. It's another handsome, best-selling artist - this time with a greased up six pack. It's... D'Angelo! His stint with Jenny Craig has paid off - he lost all that weight and is hot, once again. He joins us in our steppers' line.

I'm clapping my hands in unison with Ne-Yo, R. Kelly and D'Angelo. You can't stay seated at a steppers' party. You can't help yourself *when the* **Cha-Cha Slide** *comes on.*

The song ends. AMAZEBALLS!

"If you come to my dressing room, I'll give you some signed CDs. They're outdated, I know - I can't seem to give them away," Ne-Yo says.

D'Angelo walks off first. "Need more baby oil," he says, and leaves the room.

R. Kelly storms off, too, with the big bag of ribs. "I guess I can eat," he says.

"What's wrong with him?" I ask Ne-Yo.

"It's been almost twelve hours," Ne-Yo says.

"Since what?"

"Since he had a teenager."

"If there are any teenage girls locked in this house, Ne-Yo, I'm going to find them and set them free!"

"There aren't any. This is an alternate reality, remember?"

"Oh, yeah, right."

"We just hire pros who look young but are legal." Ne-Yo says, "I swear he's a vampire. If he doesn't get sated, he gets hungry and mean. Thank Goddess you brought dinner."

Ne-Yo walks me down a dark hall and into his dressing room. I'm surprised when he opens the door. His trademark hats hang on the walls, a flat screen TV and a book shelf filled with Criterion Collection DVDs.

"Is that, *is that Todd Rundgren I hear*?" I ask.

"**Saw The Light**, yeah? I have it on vinyl," Ne-Yo answers.

Ne-Yo likes Todd Rundgren?

"This is one of those songs you could write an entire movie around," I say.

"Are you a writer?" Ne-Yo asks.

"Yes!" I answer, feeling slightly more confident about who I am after successfully escaping sodomy in Cat Power's dressing room. I walk up to the wall next to the hats and see Ne-Yo's multiple gold and platinum records.

He takes another vinyl album out, Sonic Youth's **Daydream Nation** to play while I browse the walls. I hear Sonic Youth's **Teenage Riot** begin. *Goosebumps.*

"What the hell, Ne-Yo!? *Lost Youth?* I mean, *Sonic Youth?* And this song, did somebody call you before I arrived?"

"I am you," he says.

"Oh, yeah, right."

I'm on a quest...I'm on a quest...

"And I have eclectic taste," he says, shrugging his shoulders.

"I was at this concert over twenty years ago. This song encapsulates *everything* I've ever felt about love and connection."

"Please, don't cry."

"Don't you want someone to just *figure you the fuck out already*? To say *you're it?"*

"Don't be ashamed of crying," he says and hands me a

tissue.

"I'm really just crying over their divorce; *Thurston and Kim,"* I deflect.

"I know, sad, huh?" he says, shaking his head.

"I thought, was convinced, that everything that I loved about myself was gone. I come here, you put on this song and I'm alive again. I start to love myself and the world around me - the possibility of things, *of dreams coming true.*"

"Never give up on your dreams!"

"Proof of the power of music, the power of Art; it moves people and transforms. Seems to be a theme in my writing."

He smiles and shakes his head while drinking a bottled water.

"I could still stay out dancing all night, watch the sun rise and still have it within me to ...give...myself," I say.

I close my eyes and listen, warming up.

"Ne-Yo, you're smart, gorgeous, talented and have an appreciation for a wide range of tastes. If I were only twenty years younger..."

"Ten," Ne-Yo says, trying to make me feel better.

I notice a framed symbol in a corner wall above the stereo.

"Is that...?"

"The Trystero Symbol, from..."

"Thomas Pynchon's book, **The Crying of Lot 49**!"

"Yeah, I like old fashioned mail."

"*Snail mail* they call it now. Me too," I say and start to smile.

"Does he influence your work?"

"Absolutely! Especially what I'm writing right now."

We stand silently, listening to the record player. The lyrics to **Teenage Riot** work their way up toward my heart.

A tear moves down my cheek as I stare at the floor. Ne-Yo puts his hand out for me to hold, but I don't move, *collecting myself.*

"Beautiful," I say, quietly, "to me, at least. The angst of young love always is. It's inextricably connected to my creating."

"When you hear this song, is there someone you want to kiss?" he asks.

I'm silent and look down at Ne-Yo's shoes - *Wing-Tips.*

"How could you *not want* to kiss or be kissed with this

song on? Thurston and Kim *demand it of you.*" I answer back, after one salty swallow, still looking at the floor.

"There's nothing like a first kiss with someone, is there?"

"Yeah," I say, shaking my head in agreement, unable to raise my eyes to his.

"*Kiss me,*" he says.

"I know I'm in a fantasy here, but you're *way* too young for me, and I don't want to be pegged a Gold Digger. I can hear Kanye West singing to me right now. It's better if we're *just friends.*"

"The friends' speech? Oh, I see," he says, "You play hard to get."

"Perhaps the hardest," I answer. "I don't allow myself to say yes."

"Start today."

"Wait, this is so weird Ne-Yo. I've never given anyone the *Friends'* speech. I've heard it, but I've never had the chance to say it. Thank you! I can cross this off my list of things to do before my birthday!"

I kiss him on the cheek, grateful for the progress I've made tonight.

The credits to **Inside the Actors Studio** pop up on the TV. A movie poster for Sam Peckinpah's **The Getaway** hangs above it on the wall.

"I love the chemistry between Steve McQueen and Ali McGraw in that movie. She was married to the most powerful Producer in Hollywood, Robert Evans, and yet she meets Steve, and that afternoon, they're ripping each other's clothes off in his trailer. Now *that's chemistry;* the power to just give someone a look and change their life forever. Steve was able to do that with Ali." I go on, "There's nothing more attractive than a man with a powerful gaze; a look that says so much, without...*without having to say anything at all."*

"They definitely had chemistry. *En fuego,* those two."

"Their characters in that film have no one else to love, but each other. That's why they're so connected."

I walk over to the DVD case. I can't believe the breadth of his taste: Fellini, DeSica, Coppola, Scorsese; my favorite Italian filmmakers!

"What do you think about Wes Anderson?" he asks.

"Rushmore!" we answer together.

Am I crazy, or do Ne-Yo and I have a connection here?

He's not just a talented singer and dancer, but...a cinephile?

"And Sofia…" Ne-Yo begins.

"Coppola?" I ask, "My *mentor*?"

"Lost In Translation."

"I feel like I'm both Bill Murray and Scarlett Johansson in that movie. How did Sofia manage that?"

"It captures loneliness and *the need for connection*."

Do we like agree on everything, Ne-Yo and I?

"I like you," he says with a smile.

"I like you too, Ne-Yo. You know, I'm an unemployed, starving artist. Maybe I could hang out here during the day and watch movies with you. Since I'm a writer, we could start our own film criticism blog?"

"I'm leaving tomorrow to begin my tour, sorry."

"It's okay. *It's hard to find a best friend after forty."*

"Hey, you still want to hear some music?"

"Love to!"

"Let me do something nice for you before you leave. Let me put on a concert - a private one. Can you stay a little longer?

Ne-Yo pops open a bottle of Cristal and pours me a glass. We walk back into the studio and he sits me down in a single fold out chair on the dance floor, facing the stage.

"Hey, Mitch, stage lights," he orders and walks behind the curtain.

I'm sitting in a chair in the middle of an empty dance floor staring at R. Kelly's stage.

"D'Angelo - You're up first!" Ne-Yo yells. "Give this white girl what she came for!"

The music starts and I hear D'Angelo start to walk on stage. It's the greatest song ever written for a man to sing to a woman about to get naked, period. **Untitled or, How Does It Feel?**

D'Angelo walks toward me, winking and smiling. He sees how uncomfortable I am and how I don't like being watched here on the empty, dark dance floor. I'm hyperventilating.

I'm dizzy, having heart palpitations. My thighs are shaking and lifting off the chair. There's no song that can ever measure up to this one....like...ever. It's D'Angelo's homage to Prince.

"I can't take anymore. You people are trying to kill me!" I

scream.

I get up out of the chair, leaving D'Angelo singing and I run toward what I think is the backyard but, instead, I run straight into clear glass doors and fall backwards.

I wake up strapped onto a gurney being rushed into an ambulance.

"What's going on?" I ask the paramedic.

"You hit your head."

"Get me off this thing!" I scream.

I undo the straps and jump off the gurney and onto the sidewalk.

"I just wanted a Steppers' party! Yes, I'm white, but so was Teena Marie and she was the Ivory Queen of Soul. I bet she had lots of them!"

"Well, Lady Tee was the first white woman to perform on **Soul Train**!" the EMT yells back before hopping into the ambulance.

The paramedics drive off. I'm safe to walk this block in Kenwood with the President's snipers overhead, but I have no idea how to get myself safely to the north side of Chicago.

A pretty young girl in pigtails and a school uniform bikes up to R. Kelly's. I must intervene.

"Hey, you're way too young to be going into that house. Please, let me ride on your handle bars to the train stop and then you can go home."

"I'm twenty-five years old, not fifteen," she tells me.

"Wait, you're the *Professional?* What skincare line do you use? You look amazing!"

"I'm a Medical student at University of Chicago and this *gig* pays my tuition."

"Wait, the elusive grad student who prostitutes herself to pay the bills? I thought you were an urban myth!"

"The pay is great and R. Kelly doesn't ask me for much. We usually just play Connect Four or Tiddlywinks. Come in the house with me, I'll call you an Uber."

I walk into Ne-Yo's dressing room again and he's on the couch watching Hayao Miyazaki's **Spirited Away**. *I'm not even going to bother telling him how much I love it. He is me and I am him.*

"You're back?" he asks, concerned.

"Someone just called me an Uber. It's hard to press numbers into a phone during a dream."

"Then, join me."

"It's a masterpiece."

"You're right about that."

"I believe in ghosts. When **Teenage Riot** played tonight well, I thought I saw one," I say. "Sometimes, a ghost can just be a past version of yourself that you've missed. I miss the younger, more passionate person."

"I believe in a collective unconscious. I'm a follower of Carl Jung."

"If I dream about someone, even thousands of miles away, I always wonder if they might be having a dream about me at the same time. Does that sound crazy?"

"No, not at all."

"I think maybe I just want to believe that."

"Not a bad wish. Like having a Steppers' party?"

"I'm pretty sure the comedienne Lucille Ball and I exchanged dreams at one point."

I smile and eat some of Ne-Yo's delicious popcorn.

R. Kelly and the Call Girl come into Ne-Yo's dressing room and join us. R likes animated films. He grabs and places one of Ne-Yo's hats on each of our heads. Just a big softee, this R.Kelly. *He won't last long in prison.* He offers us all a piece of Hubba Bubba gum and we embark on a bubble blowing contest which the Call Girl wins.

"He's in a much better mood now," I whisper to the Call Girl, who sits on the love seat reading a giant book about Orthopedics.

R scares easily during the scene in **Spirited Away** where the parents eat so much that they turn into giant pigs. He covers his eyes.

I wish my parents were here. They are *spirits* now. Just like in the movie.

Ne-Yo gets my attention and whispers into my ear, "Such a baby."

"I totally relate to the whole over-active imagination thing in **Spirited Away**," I whisper. "My parents gave me a lot of time alone to fantasize growing up –at the racetrack, the pool room, sitting in the car, for hours. I always imagined I was somewhere or someone else."

"Yes, you do have a big imagination," Ne-Yo says, laughing and punching me in the shoulder.

"Since it's obvious there's a Japanese theme here, I might as well tell you that my first kiss was with a half-Japanese boy. It happened the night before the **Live Aid** concert, summer of '85."

"What's **Live Aid**?" Ne-Yo asks.

"See, I knew you were too young for me."

R takes his hands off of his eyes and offers me some Jelly Bellys. "President Ree-gan's favorite," he tells us.

"It's not pronounced like that," I say.

R frowns.

Ne-Yo whispers, "Maybe if you stopped being such a know-it-all, you would have more friends."

"I'm not a know-it-all. Can't finish crossword puzzles and I'm lousy at standardized tests," I whisper back

Things happen fast in alternate realities and my Uber arrives.

R, Ne-Yo and The Med Student/Call Girl all stand in the

doorway outside of the mansion to say goodbye.

"Thanks guys. That guys. That was fun," I say.

"Here you go!" The Call Girl says, handing me a card. "I'm going into plastic surgery."

I roll my eyes at her.

"Text me if you're at Tisch this summer," Ne-Yo, my buddy, tells me. "I'll get you tickets to our show at the Garden."

"And if there's time, a quick flick at the Angelika?" I tease. I walk down the driveway to the waiting car. I hear R. start to sing, *"Who's got a birthday tomorrow?"*

"Me! It's going to be *my birthday!"* I yell, waving goodbye.

"Hey, Eddy, would you write a letter to the judge on my behalf?" R asks.

"You might be a great singer, R., but your ass is going back to jail. Sorry!"

I shut the Uber door and the car screeches off. I take Ne-Yo's hat off.

"Just drive," I say. Not a single car to be seen on the highway this time of night.

I grab my headphones out of my purse and, in a mad rush, play Sonic Youth again. I've been waiting all night for this moment; a moment alone, with my imagination in the **Daydream Nation.**

My heart races with the guitar and the drums. I unbutton my blouse and roll down the window. I want to scream. Goddam **Teenage Riot**. Goddam lost youth. Did I recapture you tonight? *Please, Goddess, let me take this fiery, rock and rollin' girl back to the present! This is the energy I miss. This is the creative energy I need!*

I dig my nails into my thighs. Wish the car could go faster, the music louder.

The street lamps on Lakeshore Drive that we pass by quickly blur, *and then, I sail overseas.*

7 LIVE LA DOLCE VITA

I do my best to blend in on the Rue Saint-Honore in a trench coat and sunglasses, drinking a *Coke Lite*. I take my binoculars and zoom lens camera out often to stare at a window above the store *Colette*. I'm trying to catch a glance of the best looking couple in the world - Marion Cotillard and Guillaume Canet. I'm stalking them and I intend on sleeping with Guillaume Canet, star of the films **The Beach**, **Joyeaux Noel** and **Last Night**, before I leave Paris. This ought to make up for the Duchovny fiasco.

My plan is simple. Once the nanny leaves the house, I show up with a croissant delivery except my croissants are filled with sleeping pills. I tie Marion Cotillard up and throw her in the nearest closet and wait patiently, naked (under my Agnes B. trench coat) for Guillaume Canet to wake up and start kissing him. *Easy Peasy Lemon Squeezy.*

"What are you doing? It looks interesting?" I hear from an older man with an Italian accent, wearing a gray cashmere coat.

"Oh, nothing," I say, trying to distract him.

Wait! Is it… it can't be! It's Marcello Mastroianni. The star of **La Dolce Vita** is sitting behind me!

"That's too bad," he says. "I'm bored just sitting here at this cafe smoking cigarettes in my Persols, looking gorgeous."

"Wow, I can't believe it's you. You're still so handsome."

"I'm Italian, you, you know. We age well."

"Aren't you...um *dead?"* I ask, trying not to hurt his feelings.

"Yes, for years now. I'm a ghost. It's the best."

"I totally get it. I believe in ghosts, spirits, and connections."

"Totally. Sophia..."

"Loren?"

"Yes! Well, she brought me back to life."

"I'm… well, you'll never believe this. I'm stalking Guillaume Canet and Marion Cotillard, the world's most beautiful couple."

"Oh, they're *that* good looking? Like Catherine and I were in our day?"

"Deneuve?" I ask.

"Of course, you idiot!"

"Any suggestions as to how to get up to their flat? How to seduce Guillaume with Marion there?"

"Marion? She played Coco Chanel, right? Oh, I'd hit that. How about we do a *tag team?*"

"I'm not sure if that's the true definition of *tag team,* but whatever works. What do you propose?"

"HELLO! I'm an actor, *like a really famous one.*"

"So, we should act?"

"Of course. I'm acting royalty, so they'll let me in, no problem. Probably so vain that they don't even know I'm dead. You, on the other hand, we're going to have to do something about the way you look."

"What's wrong with the way I look?"

"You're a woman, but you don't show it. We need… we need Sophia. She'll know what to do with you."

"I wonder if she can also teach me the secret to Napoli pizza crust?"

"She keeps Bolognese on the stove for me; *can't get a decent one here in Paris.*"

We arrive at Sophia's flat on the Champs-Elysees. She opens the door in a negligee and see-through robe.

I avert my eyes.

"Marcello," she says seductively and frowns when I pop out from behind him.

"Hi Sophia, I'm Eddy Sass. I like...*love your work.*"

"Marcello, I told you no Americans for three ways!"

"No, not her. She needs our help. Make sure to let Catherine up. I scheduled a nooner with her."

Insatiable, Marcello is.

"Wow, you really have an active sex life for such, maturity? And the fact that you're a ghost!"

"I'm Italian, *do we need to go over this again?"* Marcello fumes, taking off his Gucci coat. "Where's my Bolognese?" he asks and heads toward the dining room.

"You might be my toughest makeover yet," Sophia barks at me. "Strip!"

Kind of strange, but I go with it.

I remove all of my clothes except for my bra and underwear and stand in the living room in front of Sophia Loren who still wears the see-through robe. *Only slightly uncomfortable.* Marcello ravenously eats pasta like a lion, pacing past us, back and forth, while still managing to puff on a cigarette.

"Not too bad," Marcello comments. "You can work with her, can't you?"

"Her bra and panties don't match and she's got a *culo* out to here!" Sophia screams.

"Sorry." I apologize.

"At least you've got *grande seni.* Now *that* I can work with!" Sophia says.

"Your Bolognese smells really good, Ms. Loren," I say.

"Don't even think about it," Sophia says sternly through her designer frames." And suck in that stomach!"

Marcello finishes his pasta and lies down on the sofa to take a nap. Sophia places new La Perla lingerie from her closet in front of me.

"You're not twenty! *You can't just take your clothes off!* There needs to be some smoke and mirrors, and most importantly, *an unveiling.* Did you not see my movie, **Marriage, Italian Style**?"

"So, is it true? You missed Marcello so much, that he came back to you as a ghost?"

"I needed him, so I called for him. When I was a young girl, starting out as an actress, he was my friend. He understands me."

"I love to think that life can come full circle."

"Marcello knows that he can be himself with me. I'm happy just watching him sleep on my sofa after eating my spaghetti. It's a great joy in my life."

Sophia finishes snapping the brasserie on.

"See, now you look like a woman. Guillaume will be Pleased," Sophia says, smiling for once.

"Sophia, I feel like a woman. Thank you. I've always felt

so uncomfortable *with...my body."*

The doorbell rings.

"Hold that thought."

"Bonjour!" says...*Catherine Deneuve!* I'm positively

dizzy. Ghosts, Sophia Loren, Catherine Deneuve? Next thing you

know, Serge Gainsbourg will show up – *and then he does!*

"Bonjour!" says the ghost of Serge Gainsbourg. I love

French pop music! I need to pinch myself.

"Did you bring the dresses?" Sophia asks.

"Yes, of course," Catherine answers.

Catherine showcases an array of dresses – Dolce and

Gabbana, Christian Dior, Valentino. They're the most feminine

andmost beautiful dresses I've ever seen.

"And the shoes?" Sophia asks.

"Yes, Serge has them. *My God, this girl has big feet!"*

"I'm tall," I say softly. "And James Joyce was known to

have a foot fetish. He wouldn't have minded them!"

"Where's Marcello?" Catherine asks Sophia.

"On the couch, sleeping." Sophia answers lovingly.

95

"Tell me something I don't know!" Catherine answers and she and Sophia giggle together.

"So, you also know he's a ghost?" I ask Deneuve.

"Well, yes, of course. He hasn't aged in years! All the luck."

"Catherine, I have SO many questions to ask you!" I'm so excited and try to calm down, *but I'm rabidly star fucking her.* "The **Umbrellas of Cherbourg** is my favorite movie musical. I, I love the whole story – boy and girl meet, fall in love – boy leaves for war and returns to find the girl has moved on, *had to move on.* Eventually, they get over one another. So, they don't end up together. It's so..."

"French?" Catherine answers.

"I loved you in **Belle Du Jour, The Last Metro**, and **The Hunger** of course. You're the sexiest vampire of all time! What's it like to make out with Susan Sarandon? Did Bowie sing on set?"

"Alright, enough of the flattery! Let's get you dressed and seducing Guillaume. He and Marion are like Marcello and I were in our time. Well, almost. No one can be *that good looking.*"

The Christian Dior clings too tightly on my butt and yet

the Dolce and Gabbana and the Valentino fit my bottom perfectly.

"Italians!" Sophia and I say in unison. Catherine rolls her eyes.

Finally, we decide on the black, strapless, lace Dolce and Gabbana. *Eat your heart out, Monica Bellucci.* Catherine teases my hair and Sophia applies my heavy black eyeliner. I look in the mirror, sucking my stomach in, and feel transported to **La Dolce Vita**. Wow. Did I fall asleep during my fifth showing of Woody Allen's, **Midnight in Paris** *or what*?

"Bellissima!" Marcello praises, waking up from his sofa slumber and lighting a fresh cigarette.

"So, what's our plan?" I ask

"We go there and say you're a journalist wanting an interview. They won't even realize I'm a ghost. They're very similar to Catherine and I when we were the most beautiful couple in the world. We were so full of ourselves; we barely knew anyone else's names but our own."

"Wait, one second, before you go!" Sophia shouts and runs to grab me her Sable fur wrap.

"Sophia, I couldn't." I say.

"Take it." Sophia orders "Every woman should have a perfect outfit at least once. Now, good luck!"

"Remember, French men like to talk dirty," Catherine instructs. "Don't be offended."

"Oh, thanks, Catherine. Guillaume could say *refrigerator* and it would still sound sexy."

"Re'frige'rateur."

"If I ever get a Hollywood studio to fund one of my films, I'll write a script just like this and both you and Sophia can star." I promise my French Fairy Godmother.

"That will be the day! *We don't share billings, Sophia and I.*"

Catherine takes a two foot tall bottle of Chanel No.5 out of her purse and lacquers my neck with it.

I'm riding on the back of a Vespa holding tight to Marcello. He has his sunglasses on and a smoke in his mouth. *We are so fucking cool.* We drive to the Champs-Elysees past the Arc De Triomphe and toward Guillaume. I can't believe I'm finally going to meet him.

We stand outside of the Second Arrondissement door of

Marion Cotillard and Guillaume Canet.

"Did you take your Viagra?" I ask Marcello, seriously.

"I'm dead you nit wit. I can go all night!"

"Okay, divide and conquer, Marcello, divide and conquer!"

Marcello knocks on the door and says something in French.

Guillaume opens the door and smiles at me. So handsome.

I hope Duchovny isn't jealous - *he's my best friend and will totally*

understand...

"Ciao! Ciao!" Marcello flirts with both Marion and

Guillaume.

"This is Eddy from America. She's here to do the

interview. Let's have some wine, shall we? Lots and lots of wine!"

Guillaume pours me a glass of red wine. My hand shakes as I

receive it.

"I love Bordeaux," I say. "Don't tell Marcello this but I like

French wine better than Italian."

"Don't tell Marion this but I like Italian women better than

French," Guillaume whispers to me, winking.

He's making a pass at me - *already?* Thank you, *Thank*

you, Catherine Deneuve and Sophia Loren!

We empty three bottles of wine *like it's a Monday night at my house* and Marcello seduces Marion with lots of Italian words ending in the letter 'i'.

"Your movie, a few years back, where you two originally met: **Love Me If You Dare**. I hope they ended up together, growing old and not dead in a cement pile, as it was suggested. Cement has been a recurring theme tonight – being *subconsciously stuck and all*. Sometimes, I need an American, happy ending."

"I love that movie." Guillaume says softly.

"So, you were the star of Fellini's **La Dolce Vita**? Wow. I'm in the presence of a true icon. If I slept with you, I would make the cover of **OK!** Magazine. It's definitely something the most beautiful woman in the world would do," Marion tells Marcello.

I can't believe she doesn't realize he's dead…Narcissist.

"You waited long enough to ask me to make love. I was getting worried." Marcello says. Marion holds Marcello's hand and they start to walk toward one of the bedrooms.

"We're French. We have an open relationship." Marion tells me.

"Divide and conquer," Marcello whispers back at me.

So, here I am, stuffed into a Dolce and Gabbana dress, drunk off of Bordeaux, sitting next to my fantasy-filmmaker-Frenchman. Too bad I don't speak his native tongue. I want to connect with this man. *I need to connect with this man.* I can't sleep with someone I don't love. Even in my dreams.

"In the movie **The Beach**, when your girlfriend leaves you for Leonardo DiCaprio, I had to use a suspension of disbelief as I can't imagine a woman *ever* leaving you," I tell the most beautiful man in the world.

Guillaume leans over to kiss me. It might be a great kiss, if he didn't taste like an ashtray.

"Mint?" I ask and offer him one I magically produce from my purse. *In alternate realities, things happen fast.*

"Follow me," Guillaume says and we walk into a sparsely decorated bedroom. He must know that I'm a minimalist and one of my pet peeves is clutter. *I'm getting turned on.* He plays **Miss Modular** from Stereolab's, **Dots and Loops** album and lights a candle. He's got moves, this Guillaume, and I like it. I know I only like him for superficial reasons; there's no deep intellectual and heart connection like the one I have with David Duchovny. I simply like Guillaume for his looks; his warm smile and smiling eyes. Can't I be shallow?

"Well, let me see you," he says with that French accent of his. *Damn, he's sexy. Slow unveiling, slow unveiling.*

I try and unzip the dress but can't reach back with my hands and nearly rip it. I don't want to owe Sophia money.

"I could use some help here," I say.

Guillaume smiles. It is such a big and happy smile, I feel warm all over. It's a sparkler that lights up the room and never burns out. I feel like I've known him for years, before tonight, but we're strangers. *I can't quite figure out what this lesson is about…To not take life so seriously? To allow myself fantasies, any fantasies, that bring me joy? To no longer qualify my desires to other people?*

Guillaume stands behind me and unzips my dress, pulling it off, leaving me standing with my La Perla set on – push up bra, panties, garters and thigh highs. Sophia and Catherine were right - *what lies beneath matters.*

Guillaume smiles and kisses my neck from behind. He

sticks his tongue in my ear – it tickles. My knees wobble *and I won't be able to stand up in these Louboutins for much longer.*

"Do you…" I say through the heavy breathing.

"Oui?"

"Do you mind if I call you a different name?"

"Pourquoi?"

He puts his right hand on my boob. *Goddess, Guillaume Canet has his hand on my boob!*

"You know, for fun?"

He turns me around and starts to kiss down the nape of my neck to my chest. I whisper the name into his ear.

"But we just met. I'm Guillaume. Don't you want to be with me?"

"I thought men liked to fantasize about other women? I like to fantasize about other men."

"But this is our first time together. You should only want me, Guillaume; the most beautiful man in the world!" He ceases his kisses.

"I don't mean to hurt your feelings, but you should know I'm not here to sleep with *you*, per se. I'm here to sleep with the ghost of someone from my youth, that you remind me of, *that's all.* To be fair, you're *much* better looking, but you share the same smile...and hair."

"So, I, Guillaume Canet, I'm not enough for your fantasy? You have to add a fantasy within your fantasy to be satisfied?"

"Well, yes. This is an alternate reality, after all! I feel less guilty projecting my desire onto you, a celebrity, than onto a real person? I have a problem with fictionalizing everyone, understand? I learned it in my childhood. Sorry!"

"You should be."

"I have satisfaction issues, like *major* ones."

"I don't think I can be the one to help you."

"Please, Guillaume, help me, before my birthday. I beg you. I've been waiting a long time for tonight and this...this fantasy."

"I don't know if I want to go through with this," he says still looking gorgeous but folding his arms together and sneering.

I pull Guillaume's arms apart and kiss him hard, passionately. I've never made the first move before, but this fantasy is important to me and I'm willing to risk almost anything to see it through…

"Listen Guillaume." I say, while sucking on his neck "Let's just do it my way, first, *with the name,* get it out of the way? Then I'll feed you some madeleines, some Viagra, and go down on you. Before you can say *'Nescafe,'* you'll be ready for round two. I'll definitely call you Guillaume in round two... I mean probably, maybe…at least *I will try to…"*

"I won an academy award. The French Oscar!"

"Listen, unless you eat a smoked salmon pizza at Spago, it's not an Oscar."

"Do you want to direct films? You sure like to tell people what to do!" he shouts at the top of his Gitanes stained lungs.

He starts to laugh, and years disappear. I smile back.

"Did you ever hear the Serge Gainsbourg?" he begins.

"Oh, my Goddess - Serge was just over at Sophia Loren's tonight!"

"Well, there's this song **Relax Baby, Be Cool.** Do you like, know how to relax?" He asks.

"Relax? *No. Never. I don't. I mean, with David Duchovny, I do…"*

"David Duchovny? From the X-Files?"

I slowly put my dress back on. *What was I thinking? Role playing with Guillaume Canet? We just met!* I grab a pillow off the bed and hit Guillame with it.

"Let's just jump up and down on your bed?"

Guillaume giggles and we start to have a pillow fight. He sings all of the French lyrics to **Cybele's Reverie -** *perfectly.* I blush every time I see his smile, with the big, fat, round wrinkles around his mouth. I have to kiss him one more time, before I leave. *Where am I headed next? Home? Have I learned enough?* "This song, it makes me feel free!" I tell Guillaume, jumping up and down on the bed.

"Me, too!" he agrees, smiling even larger, eyes twinkling, pulling me back down on the floor to dance like **Austin Powers**.

Laying on his now destroyed bed linens, catching our breath from jumping, he holds my hand. I allow this.

Stereolab's **Percolator** plays. It's all in French. Guillaume whispers the words into my ear while I stare at the ceiling and drift off...

"You're somewhere else, aren't you?" he asks, frustrated.

I don't answer. He's right. I am somewhere else...This is what I learned from my dead parents. How to escape reality. Even alternate reality! I remind myself to stay *present.* I focus again and put my guard down.

"This song, it's like you...bubbling..." he says softly.

He shakes his head and leans over me.

"I get it now," he whispers into my ear.

He lifts the bottom of my black lace dress up to my waist with both hands. I just lie there, trying to keep myself present. He gently climbs on top of me.

"*Essayez et vous de `tendre.*" Guillaume whispers.

He kisses my hand...and up my bare arm...

I am motionless.

I say the name.

I open my eyes and look up at his. We are connected – *finally.*

Then, I shudder, and moan, beneath him, hearing him say *my* name.

To name it is to give it life.

"How was Marion?" I ask Marcello on the Vespa ride back to Sophia's.

"Beautiful, beautiful girl," he tells me, "But she submits too easily...like Catherine. I like my women to have a little fight in them first, you know, like Sophia. Don't tell her I said this, but I think *she's the perfect woman.*"

I smile and kiss Marcello on the cheek.

"How did it go?" Sophia asks, opening her door.

I don't answer her.

"A fantasy is fun to have, but it can never live up to the real thing, can it?" Sophia says.

"Did you ever want to be perfect for someone?" I ask the high priestess/sage of all Italian women.

She frowns hearing this.

"If you don't think you're perfect now, you never will."

"Everything about me tonight was perfect - my clothes, my hair, my makeup, the boy. I feel prettier now than I did twenty years ago, but..."

Sofia feeds us Bolognese and then the three of us cuddle up on her sofa to watch a **CSI Miami** rerun. We're snuggled under thick, *Pratesi* Italian cashmere blankets that remind me of home. With so many ghosts around, the room stays pretty cold.

Marcello falls asleep quickly with his perfect head of black hair in Sophia's lap, curled up like a little boy. She kisses his forehead.

"Eddy, its okay for me to believe in ghosts, to love them. But, you're so young. I know you think you're not, but you are! Far too young to live in the past. Look forward, my beauty. Let your birthday be the start of your *prime.*"

"I like Guillaume and not just because he's the most beautiful man in the world but I tried hard, Sophia, but we couldn't connect. Not really…not the way I want to – *like with Duchovny.*"

"Be patient and *allow.* When it happens, you'll know it."

"When did you realize you loved Marcello?" I ask.

"Besides the fact that he's gorgeous?"

"Yes."

"I love everything that comes out of his mouth! Look at us, here, on the sofa. Me in a Mumu and him snoring. This is what the most beautiful couple in the world is supposed to look like. *This is La Dolce Vita, Eddy.*"

Sophia smiles and kisses the sleeping Marcello again.

I finally understand why I'm here.

Sophia nods off, next, happily in love with her ghost.

I attempt to quietly lift myself off of the sofa to sneak another bowl of pasta before I leave but Sophia grabs my arm as I try to get up.

"Stop eating so late!" she yells and smacks my *culo* like my grandmother used to, before falling back asleep beside me.

I settle back onto the sofa, and stare out of the window and onto the flickering, evening streetlights on the Champs –Elysees.

Lesson learned: *The Sweet life is today.*

8 GET MADE

Fritz was a black, short haired, standard size Dachshund, hailing from a puppy farm in downstate Illinois. As a puppy, he was left alone between the hours of noon and seven, while my father was at the racetrack.

As a result, Fritz suffered from an abandonment complex and was insecure. Even the cat he shared the house with, *Eight Ball,* bullied Fritz - even though she weighed half as much as he did. The first time I took Fritz to the dog park to meet other dogs, he peed himself and clung to my leg or the fence, "nerves" we called it. We teased Fritz about his weight - *he could put on extra pounds rather quickly* - and joke, right in front of him, too – *This dog is not an Alpha!*

Then, something changed; something *extraordinary.* At

age five, or thirty-five human years, Fritz, also known as "Little Pup," returned from a road trip to Vegas with my father, a different dog. No longer did he let the cat bully him, no longer did he cry for my father during the hours of the racetrack. If he wanted to take a dump on the kitchen floor, *he would.* He'd give you a look, too, across the room, after you caught him that said *"You gotta problem with that?"* There was no leg, nor species he wasn't afraid to hump. He had been transformed. His body, possessed by an alien.

"What's going on with your dog?" I asked my Dad, as Fritz gave me a once over while watching **Jeopardy** on the couch.

"He got *made,*" my Dad answered, not even turning his head to speak to me, still shouting answers toward the projection TV on the wall and a giant Alex Trebek.

"What?" I asked, confused. This was one of those times when I was faced with something unbelievable as a Pool Hustler's Daughter; so unbelievable, that my friends would never understand. No wonder it's so easy for me to live in a fantasy world.

"He got *made* – now leave him alone," my father yelled, still looking ahead at the TV and not at me.

"What happened on that trip?"

"What is The Battle of the Bulge?" my father answered, correctly, clapping his hands with Fritz barking beside him in approval.

The perks of Fritz being *made* included double cheeseburgers and chili fries from Steak and Shake, and a permit to enter any building in the U.S. No, he wasn't a Seeing Eye dog; Fritz was short and nearly drown trying to swim with his hot dog body and tiny legs. He barely weighed thirty pounds.

After being *made,* Fritz even started to understand orders my Old Man barked at him – *in Italian.*

I wanted to be like Fritz. I, too, wanted that control, that power, that confidence; a 'Take Me As I Am' attitude. I wanted *my* abandonment complex to go away. I'd been bullied my entire life and enough was enough. If I didn't fix things now, and set my life on a new course, like Fritz had, I never would. If Fritz, aka "Little Pup," a Weiner dog, could get made, *then, fuck it, so could I.*

I show up to the cigar shop on the south side of Chicago with a Sicilian anchovy pizza, a lime Jello mold and some Peronis.

"For Vito," I say, and am waved toward Vito - a bald guy with a potbelly reading the sports section wearing alligator shoes.

I walk into a backroom filled with fat guys with pinky rings smoking cigars.

"What do you want, kid?" the Capo, Vito asks. He's secretly grateful for the interruption as he's losing this hand.

"I want to get *made,*" I announce, handing over lunch to Vito's crew.

"Shut your mouth! You're glad we just did a sweep for bugs this morning!" he yells.

"She wants *to get made?*" Mikey, a younger, muscle type in an Adidas track suit asks, laughing. I think we're fifth or sixth cousins.

"Get the fuck outta here!" Vito jokes, and the rest join him, laughing.

"I'm serious, Vito. I'm about to have my *half century* birthday and I need to know what the power of being *made* feels like. My father's dog got made a few years ago and he gets everything he wants! Filet Mignon, Halloween costumes, Christmas gifts, and he never hears the word *no* from anyone. *He's a dog!*"

"Wait, you mean to tell me, your Dad's got a *made* dog?"

"Yes, that's what I'm trying to tell you."

"It's a Doberman, a German Shepherd?" Vito asks.

"Well, it is German….*a Dachshund…*" I start to explain.

"You mean a *Weiner Dog? A fuckin' hot dog?*"

All the guys at the table start laughing. Vito is turning red with anger.

"Some people do refer to the breed as a *hot dog*, but it didn't happen in Chicago. It was in Vegas, and I know better to ever question what happens in Vegas," I say.

"What happens in Vegas stays in Vegas!" Mikey jokes.

"Exactly!" I say.

"Just because a dog got made, doesn't mean I'm going to let a broad get made. It's not what we do. A woman can't get made," Vito explains.

"Vito, first off, I appreciate you referring to me as a Woman," I say.

"No sweat," Vito answers.

"But, you've failed to acknowledge the character 'Lucky,' Jackie Collins's Mob Boss Heroine in her book entitled, **Lucky.**"

I throw the Jackie Collins paperback on the poker table.

"Sorry, I don't care, for soft porn without pictures," Vito argues, throwing the book back at me.

"Wait, you mean to tell me you'll let a *dog* get made?" I scream.

"It's a *boy* dog." Mikey adds.

"A dog get made, *but not a woman?"* I scream louder, *Italian and all.*

"Why do you think the Mafia even came into existence? To get away from women! Italian women are *fuckin' nut jobs* if you hadn't noticed!"

"Italian women are the most wonderful, caring, giving, sexy women on the planet!" I yell.

"Okay, I'll agree with the sexy part, but they're also the most dangerous." Vito adds. "I brought a stray cat home one day and my mother threw it in the river. You know how Italian women are about cats…" he complains, almost crying.

"They think they are witches," I answer, softly.

"It was just a cat!" he mourns, tearing up.

"You should have known better," I say softly.

"That's what I'm talkin' about. You're all friggin' crazy! My wife, my daughter, my sister, my cousins, my nieces - all crazy! The only kick I get out of life is here at the cigar shop hiding," he hollers, slamming his hand down.

"Fine, I feel you. But you've got to honor my request. My Gram babysat you when you were a kid. *She wiped your ass, Vito."*

"You're not even from the neighborhood; you're not even one hundred percent Italian," he says.

"So?" I say, shrugging my shoulders.

"You talk funny," Mikey butts in.

"What you see before you if the result of a Lincoln Park address, three scholarships, ten Jewish mothers and elocution lessons from Blair Warner from the TV show **The Facts of Life**." I say, smiling.

"You ever threaten anyone?" Vito asks.

"Well, I did send a boy a dead fish," I answer.

"That's good, I like that. You've got balls. You inherited something from your Grandmother," Vito says, relieved.

"But, did you whack him?" my cousin asks.

"Whack off? Yes, many times," I answer, thinking back, and smiling.

"No, did you *kill* him?" my cousin asks again, louder.

"No, unfortunately, he retaliated with a dead gerbil and we made up," I say.

"Fine, fine," Vito says, "You want to *feel* like a made man."

"Woman," I correct.

"Woman," Vito continues, "Then I'll give you the hardest job there is."

"Do I have to kill anyone with an ice pick?" I ask.

"No, it will require guts, though. You need to collect the till from the Bingo Hall."

"The Bingo Hall? What's so hard about that?" I ask.

All the guys at the table laugh.

"The last guy we sent there hasn't been heard from in months," Vito says.

"Why do they pay you?" I ask.

"Well, who do you think hangs curtains, fixes leaky pipes, gets the best date at the wedding hall? We do," Mikey explains.

"Well, how much do they owe?" I inquire.

"Two grand," Vito answers.

Okay, I can do this, my Gram was the Queen of the Bingo Hall, she was a... *legend.* "Easy!" I tell the guys.

"Easy?" Mikey laughs, *"wait til you meet Bertha."*

"Who's Bertha?" I ask

"She's in charge. Everything goes through her."

"Bertha can count cards. Don't ever play poker with her," Mikey says.

"Fine, done," I commit. "I'll get the money tonight."

"Luck with that," Vito snickers. The rest of the guys all laugh.

"Bring brass knuckles!" Mikey shouts, before I slam the door.

I arrive at the church bingo hall at 7:00 sharp. I wish my Gram was here - my Gram - *the toughest Broad I ever knew.*

"I'm here to see Bertha," I tell an old lady with bifocals on and grey, polyester pants pulled up to her neck.

"Which one?" she answers me, still popping out her pull tab tickets, hoping for a winner.

"How many Berthas are there?" I ask.

"Two. *Big and Little.*"

"Who's in charge here?" I ask

"That would be Little Bertha, and she's in her office. She expecting you? She's very busy."

"No, but I'm from the neighborhood," I say.

"You sound like you're from England or something."

"No, I'm not from England, I'm from forty blocks away. It's called the *North side*."

"But you don't live *here*?" she says, laughing at me.

"No, I don't. But three generations before me did; were baptized in this church."

"Fine, go see Little Bertha, but don't tell her I sent you," she says and walks off, pulling out a long Moore cigarette out of her blue, pleather cigarette case, and lighting it with a Zippo.

As I walk through the Bingo Hall to get to the cafeteria and get to Little Bertha, I wave and kiss numerous cousins, aunts and uncles.

They think I talk funny, too. I walk through the hall behind the cafeteria. I remember my grandmother's order at Bingo every Tuesday – coffee.

"Keep pouring the sugar in, till the stirrer stands straight up."

Once I get to the dark, dank, furnace room, I'm nervous. I've never asked anyone to give me money before, much less an old lady from the Bingo Hall.

What happened to the last Mob guy they sent here? Why is her office next to the furnace?

I see an old timey TV tray table filled with piles of small bills cash and an exposed fire from the furnace, which makes me start sweating. There's a light bulb hanging from the ceiling and I wonder if I'll be interrogated again. The church calendar hanging on the wall is dated 1979. There's a framed picture of the nineteen seventies TV Detective **Baretta**. Jimmy Durante is playing on an eight track tape which signals it's Christmas.

A very old woman in a shawl is sitting in a wheel chair. Her legs are covered with a lap blanket and she's drinking a can of Ensure out of a straw. She's watching the **Carol Burnett Show**.

Okay, I think I just met Big Bertha.

There's a younger, shorter woman, as tall as she is wide, in a brown pantsuit counting cash in white high-top Reeboks.

"What do you want?" The younger, shorter one asks.

"Hi, I'm here to see Bertha - *Little Bertha*."

"Who's asking?" retorts this same woman, who has beady black eyes. I'm guessing she's Sicilian.

"I'm here on behalf of Vito...from the cigar shop," I say.

"Vito sent you? Oh, he's getting soft. What does he want? His till? I already told him that I expect more for my money. I've got a lot of old ladies to support in this parish. They need insulin, support hose and free cable. It's not like I spend it on myself."

"Well, you sound like a nice person, Bertha. A fellow feminist. So, hopefully you'll *help a sister out* and understand that I need to bring money to Vito so I can get *made* – before my birthday."

"Laid?"

"No, *made! But I wouldn't mind that, either.*"

"Why do you want to get *made,* and why do you talk so funny?" Little Bertha asks.

"Well, my Dad's dog got *made* and I've noticed no one bullies him anymore. I'm tired of being a pushover. I...want..."

"Balls?" She asks. "You're not Cinderella. You don't need a *fat fuck* like Vito who thinks he's a King *to "dub" you anything.* Stop relying on people to give you permission! Decide who you are and that's it *wit chu now–* you're done. *Get the fuck out, please – you're making me miss my count.*"

"You make it sound so easy, Bertha. It's just that my..."

"Bark is bigger than your bite?" she says.

"Exactly."

"Nobody takes you seriously?"

"God, Bertha, how did you know?"

"You can scream all you like, Italians are good at that, but if you don't *act* on your threats... If you don't make someone afraid of what you *might* do - what they might lose – you'll get nowhere, and they won't respect you."

"Well, how do I fix this? I can't imagine entering the second half of my life *still* being a pushover. When I think of all the times I sold myself short, I want to hurt someone. I mean, I'm carrying around a lot of anger. It's...not good...*for my stomach.*

I don't want to end up with ulcers like Cat Power."

I look down on the floor, feeling my blood begin to boil, but putting a lid on it, like I normally do.

"Nine times out of ten, a person who jumps off a building wouldn't - *if they could push somebody else off."*

"That's so weird. My Dad used to tell me that all the time."

"*What you need* is to even the score. Even the score and *then* you can have healthy relationships."

"You sound like *Bridgeport Brene Brown* preaching boundaries."

"Boundaries, yeah, *but Italian-style. "*

"How do I *even the score?* I started being bullied as a toddler on the bus to Preschool. I mean, this might be a long list."

"What's your last name?" she inquires.

I tell her.

"You're Katie B's granddaughter?" she asks, excited.

"Yep, that was my Gram."

"You know she was my hero? She literally saved my mother's life - Big Bertha."

The mute old lady in the wheelchair lifts her cane a few

inches off of the floor in agreement.

"My father, he drank. He beat my mother up so bad one time that her eye popped out of its socket. Your grandmother popped it back in and nursed her back to health. She taught me to never let anyone mess with me - *ever.*"

"My Gram taught you - that? I'm jealous. I didn't grow up on the south side so I didn't hang out with her much until I was out of college and she made me take her to Bingo every week. I was in my twenties and extremely lonely. She made me feel better about myself. She was old and so strong. I was young and so weak."

"Then, you've got to know the story about her and your Aunt? The one who got picked on in grade school? The other girls called her fat?" Little Bertha asks, "That's what I want for you."

"You want me to hit a bully from the third grade?" I joke.

"I want you to stick up for yourself. Now write down a list of every single person who messed with you."

"But Bertha, these people only treated me this way because *I let them.* I know that now."

Bertha places a piece of paper and a Bic pen and front of me and points with her finger.

"And if you leave anybody out - if I catch you lying…"

"I'll make the list, I'll make the list!"

"Gas up the Impala!" Bertha tells one of her underlings in the kitchen. "And throw some Ensures in a tote bag for my mother."

We exit the Bingo Hall that night with a *hit list.* I climb into the Chevy Impala, bracing myself for our impending crime spree across the continental U.S. Little Bertha claimed that retirement from the Sanitation Department bored her. Since quitting smoking a few years back and gaining over one hundred pounds, she was addicted to Monster Energy drinks and was an adrenaline junkie now. Her biggest regret was that she never got a chance to be a cage fighter. Her favorite TV show growing up was **Baretta** - a show about a detective in New York who *also* drove a Chevy Impala and owned an exotic bird. What made **Baretta** special was his use of disguise. Little Bertha took disguises very seriously when she went on crime sprees like this one.

We drive deep into the Chicagoland Area, Little Bertha

dressed as a man in a FBI suit. She reminds me of Chaz Bono. Little Bertha decided a long time ago who she was. I admire her.

First, we find the boys who teased me on the bus to nursery school every day and throw water balloons at their heads from a nearby roof. One of the greatest assets to our operation is Big Bertha as she possesses the coveted *Handicapped Parking placard.* We easily slide in and out of any parking lot.

Next, we find the short girl in Catholic school from third grade, who stepped on my feet on the steps during dismissal. We spike her morning Java Mocha Chip Frappuccino with Ex-Lax.

Next, we break into my old office, where I had worked for fifteen years. When I tell Bertha I'm afraid of the police showing up, she tells me *'I own this town'* and downloads a virus onto the company computer which sends a double penetration porno video to every client, vendor and personal email.

The West Coast is a big blur. I don't eat fast food so I'm subsisting on mixed nuts. Also, Little Bertha drives in 4-5 hour stints until the car tank is nearly empty, so I barely drink anything as bathroom breaks are out of the question. We place a mirror under Big Bertha's mouth every so often to check if she's still breathing.

The South flies by rather quickly. Little Bertha is nothing but efficient, but she does allows me a Cajun burger at the Port of Call restaurant on Esplanade in New Orleans. I wash it down with a thirty-six ounce Monsoon drink filled with seven types of rum and fall off of my stool at the bar. I throw up on the bartender. She tips the guy a *hondo* for the trouble and asks me what's wrong.

"I made a lot of mistakes here, during college," I confess.

Bertha's dressed in a ten gallon hat, denim jacket and green lizard shit kickers she picked up in Houston. She puts a cold compress on my forehead.

I continue, "College was supposed to be a fresh start for me, but it wasn't. I made some great friends, but people still didn't take me seriously."

I black out.

When I wake up, seventeen hours later, we're almost in the Garden State. Little Bertha is dressed up as Detective Charlie Chan now. So not PC. She must watch a lot of old movies with her mother. It's embarrassing to look at, but, strangely makes me crave dumplings at Joe's Shanghai in NYC's Chinatown.

I chug a bottle of water.

"You're in the middle of your catharsis. Just like Stephen Daedalus in James Joyce's **Portrait of The Artist as a Young Man**."

"You've read James Joyce? That's one of my favorite books. A gluttonous, sexually repressed Catholic, needing to get as far away as possible from family to become an artist. Feels familiar."

"The first step of the catharsis is facing the truth. The second step is forgiving yourself. You've been taking your anger out *on yourself.* Stop that! I'm all for being responsible for yourself and not playing the victim, but don't gloss over this stuff anymore. Your friendships will suffer."

"I did gloss it over; I never wanted anyone to hate me. You know I've never broken up with someone or ended a friendship? Oh! But I did just give the *'friends'* speech to Ne-Yo. Progress?"

"You're a people pleaser. *And how far did that get you?"*

"Not far at all. It's why I'm stuck."

"Well, less stuck, than when you started this quest. William Faulkner talks about people carrying around debt books stamped

with generational family debts. Yours is stamped full and you feel ashamed."

"My parents raised me far away from all of that, in the best neighborhoods, sent me to the best schools…"

"But at the end of the day, your father is still a pool hustler. He *lived* in the underworld. You're just visiting."

"Maybe that's why I always felt like I had to try harder."

"You feel you'll never be able to do enough to be accepted and to be loved. Free yourself from this guilt, this burden you feel just because you're different. *Being different makes you interesting.* It's not up to you to pay your family debt. It's an impossible task that keeps you from being you. You don't need to change anything tonight. Just be more of yourself – *own it."*

"Thank you, Bertha. Trying to pay that debt was a Sisyphean task and made me feel like I was less deserving than everyone else."

"If you're a writer, then what do you write about?"

"Not being alone in the world."

"That's how I feel when I read Rachael Ray's **Thirty Minute Meals**."

"I invented friends when I was little and lonely. I guess I'm still inventing them."

"Tonight, for learning purposes, it's fine. But *that's it for you. Real people love you – real people will love you.* You're enough just as you are and have nothing to prove to anyone."

Little Bertha takes pity on me and lets me grab a Hoagie in New Jersey. The delicious mix of salted pork and olive oil soothes me in a multitude of ways, like my baby blanket.

We get to New York City and are quick and witty. It doesn't take much to ruin somebody's day here. Bertha lets me sit in Bryant Park and watch the ice skaters while sipping hot chocolate. It's one of my favorite places in the city. I came here as a young woman, once or twice a year, and sat for hours, reading or writing, hoping to make a friend. I admire the white lights. I feel like I've earned a rest. The list I wrote for Little Bertha has finally been completed.

At sunset, I wake up in the Impala, hoping I'm not Icarus, heading too close to the sun, and wonder how many more miles till Chicago.

Little Bertha is wearing a wig with yellow dreadlocks and

gold teeth in her mouth frightening me like Madonna did. I'm dressed in a French Maid costume – for no reason - *other than I always wanted to fucking wear one. Own it!*

"Sanitation Department is totally Gangsta!" Bertha screams out of the window, while blasting NWA into the Midwest winter air.

We exit the Dan Ryan Expressway, nearly home. Little Bertha hands me a McDonald's coffee from the Drive-thru. It's comforting and reminds me of my parents. They might be dead, but I still want them to be proud of me. My Dad begged me to stand up to bullies, and I never did. He was right, I just wasn't brave enough to do it back then. *But I am now.*

"My present to you, Katie B.'s granddaughter, for your birthday, is a clean slate." Bertha says, "The next fifty years are up to you. But don't let us down. *All of us are counting on you,"* she says, making me miss my father. I hope I see him for a moment tonight.

"I won't," I say.

"The next time the pushover in you is about to give in, think to yourself, *What would Little Bertha do? What would your*

Gram do?"

My jaw unclenches and my shoulders settle into my back nicely.

"I haven't felt this relaxed in a long time," I tell her, "Not since I spent the night with David Duchovny."

"No more bottling yourself up."

I step out of the car and onto the street. *"No more. I swear. Thank you, for everything, Bertha."*

I stand alone on the snow covered sidewalk in front of my childhood home. I feel light – so light - *as light as a snowflake –* perfect and original – floating peacefully in the wind.

9 GO TO THE PROM

I notice him immediately. He's the one guy in class who finds a way to offend everyone in his vicinity, in a non-menacing way, then smiles and acts self- deprecating to level the playing field.

His name is Sam Schulman, future all around awesome man/boy *and I am going to the senior prom with him.*

"Age difference, what age difference?" I answer Sam, as he tries to catch his breath after I jump out of the soccer team storage locker that I've been hiding in, since the end of their game. I enjoy dramatic entrances. Sue me.

"I mean, I don't have a date yet, but I could ask someone," he says.

"Listen, you're only eighteen-years-old. You're going to have lots of these type of events. I am going to be *really old* soon. I need to do this - *with you.* You're kind of, well, cool." I say.

"Cool, you think I'm cool?" he asks, still sweat on his brow under his head band post-game, staring at my breasts.

"Yes, like the coolest guy in your class; or at least the most original one. I can't think of a better guy to go to the prom with.

"Nobody would ever believe me if I told them this at college, or at my own wedding years from now…"

"See, you're thinking ahead. I always do. You can't be the most interesting boy in your class without doing something *just like this*. And besides that, I have a great coke connection."

"You do?" Sam asks.

"Yeah, *Steve McQueen.*"

"Steve McQueen, the filmmaker?" Sam asks again.

"Hello! The film star," I answer.

"Really?"

"He's a ghost friend of mine, don't ask. Marcello Mastroianni introduced me. He's a ghost, too, FYI. *Anyway, Steve gets the best shit."*

"Cool."

"So, you're like totally okay with an over forty-year-old woman going to the prom with you who occasionally talks to and/or buys drugs from ghosts?" I ask.

"Yes, I'm okay with it," he answers, smiling devilishly.

I show up to the mall of my youth and find the North Beach Leather store replaced by Yankee Candle Company. DAMN! Must procure leather mini dress on EBay. Instead of a tanning bed, I have a spray tan. I book a limo and a room at the Four Seasons post-prom. At the very least I can watch "Movies Still In Theaters" later.

Going to the prom has had very little impact on my life as a woman, on my self-confidence. Just ask my therapist(s) - *we're all in agreement on this.*

Every time I pass by the teen cocktail dress section of any Department Store, I'm reminded that I didn't go to the prom.

Now, technically I did go to the Four Seasons that night, but I didn't walk *into* the prom. From outside of the door, I saw my friends laughing and dancing with someone in a tuxedo beside them, turned around, and left.

When I show up to Sam's parents' house that night, they're concerned. Sam's thrilled. An older woman and a Shiksa – Jackpot!

I don't even get out of the car when the limo pulls up in front of his house. I just wave. Steve McQueen and I are in the middle of an intense chess game, and I don't want to lose my concentration - or to have Mr. and Mrs. Schulman notice their son is hanging out with the celebrity undead.

Sam, high off the power of messing with his parents' minds, hops into the limo and all of a sudden, starts screaming.

"AHH! Is that...? Am I seeing a ghost?" he yells.

"Sam, stop acting like such a star fucker. Steve may be the greatest box office star of the seventies, but he's just a normal guy. Likes to drink Bud and play the ponies." I pause, "Steve, this is Sam, Sam this is Steve McQueen."

Sam collects himself, taking a deep breath and shakes his hand. He braces for the cold. "Steve is dropping us off at dinner."

"Why don't you let Steve take you to the prom? I mean, he's so much cooler than me?" Sam asks.

"I'm attracted to Steve, yes, what woman isn't? I mean, come on, *he literally melts your panties off with his laser beam blue eyes.* But we have no connection as artists, you know, not much to talk about. He's pretty quiet and I love to hear a man talk; especially when it's tailored to get under my skin." I pause, "But most importantly, well, Steve is a ghost. I don't want to cause that kind of a scene." I continue, "Women *do* like it when a man stares at them, but in the right way, the way Steve does, there isn't an ounce of sap to it. It's a serious moment, and he makes a woman feel like a woman. You should learn from it."

We walk into Gibson's, the Rush Street Steakhouse. It's filled wall to wall with old men and young girls. I'm also with someone thirty years younger on my arm. *I should make the cover of Ms. Magazine for this.*

"How about some oysters and vodka?" I ask Sam, who is about to check into his phone. I grab it.

"Listen, if I see you take this out, while I am talking to you, I will throw *you*, and *it*, out the fucking window."

Sam looks scared. Poor thing has already had to accept the existence of ghosts in the world.

"I'm sorry. I've a had a hard time, not scaring men away with my death threats. It's a Sicilian thing. Please, let's have a drink."

The male, bow-tied bartender, hands us over two Stoli vodka rocks with twists and a dozen oysters.

"Here." I say, putting an oyster shell up to Sam's mouth.

"Is this an aphrodisiac?" he asks. "I definitely know it's not kosher."

"It's delicious."

"But I mean, is it going to give me hard-on?" he whispers.

"No, don't be ridiculous." I say, forgetting how self-conscious a boy is, and why I prefer men. But I had to make a concession to finally go to the prom.

We finish the oysters and I wipe Sam's mouth with my napkin. I have to stop mothering him. He's my prom date, not my child.

"So, if you don't mind my asking, why didn't you go to prom?" asks Sam.

"Well, Sam, to start with, I didn't have a date…"

"Why not?"

"Well, I was a lot different back then. For one thing I was *painfully shy*. My parents, who were divorced, had polar opposite philosophies when it came to me and my romantic life."

"Like, what?"

"Well, my mother hated men. She wanted to prove that a woman could thrive without a man, without sex."

"Yikes."

"I was her poster child, to be paraded in front of my father, to punish him. If I even mentioned I liked a boy, she'd roll her eyes at me."

"And your father?"

"Well, when he wasn't dating teenagers or prostitutes, or, teenage prostitutes, he was telling me that I did everything wrong when it came to being a woman. He demanded that I follow his very strict rules as to how to "land" a boyfriend. And if I didn't follow these rules, I was destined to be *alone* the rest of my life. The pressure was... too much! All I really wanted was to remain alone and get both of my parents off my back."

"And did you follow your father's rules?"

"I tried – barely – but again, I was shy. I came out of my

shell, *eventually."*

"And prom night?"

"My Dad screamed that there was *no way I could go to prom by myself, without a date.* It wasn't *natural.* He said it was going to fuck me up the rest of my life."

"And was he right?" Sam asks.

"Well, we're here tonight, aren't we?"

"We are"

"I'm...different now...Plus - *and don't quote me on this,* because I'm not entirely sure, but I think I might have children somewhere. The idea keeps fading in and out of my head. Anyway, *I wouldn't want them to think their mother is a loser."*

Sam and I step out of the elevator of the Four Seasons Hotel, walking past the large flower arrangements consisting of fuchsia Peonies and fragrant, white Lilies. We stroll past the water fountains and across gold and navy paisley carpets.

When we get to the ballroom, Sam walks ahead of me and through the door.

Once inside, he turns around, to see me. I'm stuck. Once

again, like thirty years' past, I can't walk inside.

"Eddy, please. You can do this. I'm going to do this with you," he says.

He walks back out of the ballroom and holds my hand.

"Better late than never." he says, "Close your eyes."

I close my eyes, and step forward.

"Now open," he says.

When I open them, there I am, I'm...at prom. And I'm not alone. And I have the best date *ever,* Sam Schulman. He, might be only be eighteen, but he's *trying* to get me...

"Drink?" he asks.

"Absolutely."

I survey the large and candlelight ballroom. I'm loving the dim lighting and promise to smile more.

Across the dance floor I see an old face, another dead one, my English teacher, the one who made me love reading, the one who noticed me, and plucked me out of the crowd. The one who wrote on my report card that I was a 'Star.'

"Dr. Stone," I say. "What a pleasant surprise.

We hug. She's flawless as usual, dressed in a grey tweed Armani skirt suit, pearl earrings and an alligator purse. She has long black hair, sapphire blue eyes, as tall and thin as any super model, brilliant, *but bat shit crazy*, in only the best of ways.

"You were… a force…to put it lightly…you changed my life…I hope you know that…You still motivate me – *every single day*!"

"I know," she acknowledges, "I just wish you hadn't waited so long to start writing again."

"Ditto. But my subject matter is self-indulgent, prose pedestrian…"

"I told you, *emphatically*. You must write while you are young. Write, write, write. What about *that* didn't you understand?"

"My early writing was garbage, even *you* know that. I had to find my voice…"

"You always hid your face behind your hair. I nearly slapped you because of it. You were pretty, didn't I tell you that?"

"You really spoke to me. I appreciate you, so much."

"Carpe Diem, Carpe Diem!"

"Carpe Diem."

"Carpe Diem is for every day. Not just for when you're young. You know what I'd be doing if I was alive right now?" she tells me, dead as dead can be, serious, "*Fucking everything*. And yes, that is a *double entendre.*"

"And that's why you're my hero," I tell her.

"I implored you to understand the importance of sex and to never overlook it. Why do you think I always spoke about it in class? I could command an audience of thousands with the suggestion. You remember every lecture that I had mentioned something of a sexual nature, don't you?"

"Of course, that was your calling card. And you were an incessant flirt."

"And that is why my students always had the best grades, became famous writers, actors and filmmakers. I knew how to get people to listen to *me*. To remember *me*. You should employ my tactics in your own writing."

"I do, I just don't want to devalue the importance of sex by talking about it too much. I will always think of it as an elusive gift."

"Eddy, it is a gift. *You, are a gift.* And fifty is nothing. Even at ninety, I could have run a marathon. *If you don't live your life, the way you imagined it, I will never speak to you again."*

"But you're a ghost."

"But I can haunt you in your dreams."

"Yes, you can. But I will never, ever fear you."

"Well, try harder. No excuses."

"No excuses," I answer her.

"Well, you know how curt I am. Off to Paris now. Gertrude Stein's salon awaits. You have no idea how we fight over the spotlight in Paris...you know... who's running the show. Gertrude's got Picasso on her side, but I've got Matisse. I told her I had my own artist's salon here in Chicago; but for some reason she thinks hers is superior...can you believe that woman? The nerve! I told her she needed to lay off the *galettes* and she told me I was a skinny bitch! I thanked her, of course, you know how hard I work to keep my youthful figure."

"Of, course."

"And the fashion in Paris, its, well, you know..."

"Oh, yes," I answer. "I was just there!"

"Let nothing stand in the way of your writing," she implores. 'And if your stuff is worthy of being a student of mine, I'll run it by Gertrude. Although, for being a lesbian, she's not that supportive of female writers...still stuck on that bastard Hemingway, like he's God or something. Personally, I think it's just penis envy. Toodles!"

"Toodles!"

And with that my teacher, hero and writing mentor dissipates through a wall, grabbing her fur stole and throwing it over her shoulder; still so very glamorous, even in the afterlife.

Sam walks up to me with a diet soda spiked with rum from his hip flask.

"Sorry," he says, "try and remember I'm only eighteen. I can't legally drink."

"Friends here?" I ask.

"Lots of friends, just…"

"Not close ones?"

"You're outgoing, Sam. I bet you'll always have lots of friends and you'll always be…in the spotlight."

146

"My outgoing behavior, well, it's usually just a decoy…
Shhh, don't tell."

"Well, I've made it to prom…because of you. You helped
me pass that threshold. Thank you, Sam, thank you."

"You don't have to."

"But, now I should be leaving. It's your night, not mine.
Tonight is for the Gen Z crowd and I'm about to enter a new
Nielsen bracket."

"But, you have to have one dance. With me? It's prom."

"Oh, that's sweet, but…"

New Order's **Temptation** begins to play.

"How?" I begin.

"DJ's your age. He also likes blow…"

"Ha!"

Sam runs out to the dance floor first. He has some rhythm
and I dance…near him…still by myself and remembering a New
Order concert in Brooklyn and how I soared that night like a
Phoenix.

I see some of Sam's teenage friends waving and
laughing at his dance moves.

I move backward, watching him a few precious moments more, and then, I walk out the door and take the hotel elevator upstairs. Room service and pay-per-view waiting. Maybe I'll even get some writing done...for Dr. Stone.

_____

A few hours later (alternate reality time) and I'm in my dark hotel room in a deep sleep. I'm the only person who can fall asleep even under the influence of stimulants. I hear a knock at the door.

"What are you doing here?" I ask, shocked, seeing Sam through the peephole. I open the door.

He says nothing. He just stares down at the carpet.

"Sam? Are you okay?" I ask again, concerned.

"*You had me at Steve McQueen's ghost,*" he tells me, looking up, and reaching for my hand.

"Sam..." I say, shaking my head, and let him kiss me, once, *no tongue,* briefly, softly. He tastes salty, like the Ocean.

"Please don't tell me you're here because of some **Harold and Maude** fetish. That would bum me out. Ruth Gordon has at least thirty years on me in that film."

I turn on the overhead light.

"Eddy, what the...?" he yells.

I turn to look at the half massacred room service tray.

"Oh, that was there when I got here. The service in this hotel is terrible."

"No, you're different, Eddy. Don't take this the wrong way, but you're *very* different. Like, decades."

He touches my face and then my hair.

"Oh, do I have chocolate cake on my face?" I run into the bathroom to look in the mirror.

"You're..." Sam begins.

"Young again," I say.

"Like my age, like..." Sam is speechless.

"Seventeen. I was seventeen the night of my senior prom. I'm younger than you. My hair. It's huge! All I did was eat some cake and fall asleep."

I look at my outfit. I grab the tag from the back of my strapless dress. It reads "North Beach Leather."

"Oh, my god! Even my voice sounds funny! Look at me, look at me! No wrinkles! And my tits are up to my neck! *Steve*

McQueen really does get the best shit!"

Sam laughs and continues to stare. His blue eyes are as bright as headlights on a foggy road.

I open up the envelope where the coke is stashed.

"It just says 'Magic' on it," he tells me.

"Steve McQueen gave us magical blow," I say, looking up at him, grinning. "Fairy Godfathers exist!"

"Why didn't I change?"

"Because you don't need to. This is your normal prom night, and Steve knows I bought and read every single biography ever written about him. I'm a dedicated fan."

"I'm glad I came back, then. You know I like you at 49, but you being *seventeen*…you're very pretty. I just want to...smell your hair."

I allow myself to listen to his compliments, digest them. I never would have as a seventeen-year-old. I do feel pretty. Why didn't I appreciate myself more when I was seventeen?

"You know, I've never kissed an eighteen-year-old before." I tell him,

"Another bonus I can cross of my list before 50."

"I'm a virgin."

"What?"

"Please don't make me go to college a virgin!"

"What? *Blow makes you say crazy things!"*

"I was coming back here to ask you to take my virginity away. Please, Eddy. I don't want to get to college a virgin! I even made a playlist on Spotify for the occasion."

He shoves his phone in my face. The play list is entitled "Sam's First Time."

"Everybody should have a soundtrack in the movie that is *their life,"* he tells me.

This kid is definitely in my head, isn't he?

"No! Absolutely not!" I yell.

"But if you're seventeen, doesn't that mean that you're..." Sam says.

"*A virgin, too.* OH MY GOD!" I scream.

"Ha, ha! You're a virgin!"

"Leave me alone, Sam, or I swear to God I'll…"

"You'll what?"

I'm surprised at my reserve. Something is holding me

back.

"I'm not as strong as I normally am. I barely said two words when I was seventeen. Especially not to boys. I guess I've come far since then."

"Listen, aren't you the one who says she'd like to see life come full circle?"

"I do, I do. I just never thought this was *an option*. Aren't there any whores at your high school who can provide this service?"

"Well, I managed to get one girl, an exchange student, to…"

Deep swallow.

"Stop! I don't want to know. I *do not* want to commit statutory rape!"

"I'm 18. If anything, *I* would be the statutory rapist since you're only 17!" he proclaims with a smile that gets wider smile and it's as if his eyes are smiling. Pretty, young eyelashes. You could ski off of them.

"Sam, I've never been naked *with* a teenager or *as* a teenager before. I don't think I'm mentally - or physically –

prepared for this."

"Steve McQueen gave you the magic cocaine for a reason, and I think *this* is it."

"Did it ever occur to you that I might want to be *attracted to you*?"

"But I thought…"

"I'm attracted to you, Sam – as a seventeen year old girl. If I was seventeen right now, and chugged a couple of Bartles and Jaymes wine coolers, I'd probably say yes."

"But you ARE SEVENTEEN RIGHT NOW!" Sam yells.

"Sam…*I'm frigid!*" I blurt out.

"What? What does that mean?"

"Giving up on the dreams and desires of my youth caused me to lose everything that made me...*me*."

"I only think of you as a writer, an artist. Does that help?"

"Listen, I hope you never have to hear that ugly word again- but it is in fact a medical condition that I suffer from. All you need to worry about at your age are wet.."

"Moist?" Sam asks.

"Vaginas," I say.

"*Like the Sonic Youth song*?" Sam asks.

"Did you Wikipedia that?" I ask, trying not to crush on this man/child.

I feel something going on *downtown. My downtown.*

"Can you excuse me a moment?' I ask.

I rush into the bathroom, close the door and look in the mirror. My face is slightly flushed, red through the fake tan. He's doing something to my body, this Sam. If being seventeen means I'm still a virgin, then it must also mean...

Sam knocks on the door.

I open it slightly, cautiously. Sam sticks his head through the opening.

"I'm turning you on, right now, aren't I? Can I see you naked?" Sam asks.

"NO!"

I slam the door in Sam's sweet, smiling face.

He's doing it. He's getting to me. I rush over to my purse and look in my wallet filled with all of my VIP club cards from thirty years ago.

I hear music from behind the door. Roxy Music. Goddam

DJs. I open the door to a dark, candlelit room. Roxy Music's **Over You** plays. This baby bastard is trying to seduce me!

*Ok, ok. Anne Bancroft was only six years older than Dustin Hoffman when they filmed **The Graduate.** I didn't enjoy being seventeen when I actually was seventeen, but I finally have the chance to enjoy it tonight. To feel like a girl. Clean slate, clean slate!*

"Take off your clothes." Sam orders as he sits on the edge of the bed loosening his tuxedo tie, throwing off his Sambas and nearly breaking the bed lamp. I look at myself in the mirror at my young and fresh virgin body. Goddam horny teenagers. Fuck! I think I'm a horny teenager too.

Sam looks me over, up and down, just like Steve McQueen would, without sap, just like I told him to. Points for listening. I am so moist right now, I feel tropical. Is my therapist taking calls from the Underworld?

"Sam, sex changes you. You deserve better than a forty-something year old *mother* desperately trying to get in touch with her younger side."

"Everything that's happening right now is supposed to

happen. Please, stop talking and take your clothes off already. I want to see you. I want to see you naked. I have a hard-on just thinking about it. You can kill me afterward if it will make you happy. Slit my throat if you like, or stab me with an Ice Pick. I know you like to threaten men you like."

Oh, God, *it's happening again.* A few times, without him even touching me.

"Sam, what's your favorite..."

"Band? The Replacements."

"Movie?"

"**Deer Hunter**, and I think the wedding scene was not too long."

"Dwarf?"

"Sleepy, of course."

"Okay, okay, Sam - YES!"

He tries to act cool, concentrated, and serious with a straight face.

"Good," he says calmly.

"But be warned…" I say. "I'm a bleeder."

When we're lying in bed together, under Four Seasons

high thread count linens, listening to Cat Power and just figuring each other's bodies out, before anyone's status officially changes, I feel connected, to this boy, who I think is a stranger, *but isn't.* I know him, like I have known Guillaume Canet, like I have known David Duchovny, like I have known Ne-Yo. We've met before. He's in my heart already, *and I love him.*

Cat Power's, **Still In Love,** plays. It's sudden, and I am *feeling it.*

"Ready?" he asks, nervously, "I don't want to hurt you," he whispers, breathing heavily, slightly afraid about what comes next.

When it's over, we are both on opposite sides of the bed… processing, lowering our heart rates, thinking; holding hands. I did it – *I literally did it* – had the cool teenage boyfriend I always wanted but never had, AND *I went to the prom*! It's a lot to process in one night, but I've cleaned this slate for good.

"What are you thinking about?" he asks, not pushy at all.

"Just how real this all feels. How it makes me remember, and miss…"

"Eddy, I…"

"Sam?"

"I love you." Sam says.

My stomach drops. *This, exactly this*, is what I always wanted to hear back then.

"I know you warned me, but...I love you," he tells me again, sitting up. "When I opened my eyes and saw you lying there, I felt it. *You changed me.*"

I look at him, this charming kid, whoever he is – me? Did I just make love to myself? My subconscious is as surreal as a Salvador Dali painting.

"I love you too, Sam," I say, sincerely.

He looks happy, happy that I love him. I make Sam happy! It's kind of the best part. Knowing that I make another person happy by being myself, or, or, at least, the younger version of me.

"You know, I wanted to be a torch singer, Sam," I say.

"I can imagine it, like Diane Keaton in **Annie Hall,**" he says, smiling. "My fave…"

"Don't even say it," I tell him.

Chan Marshall, aka Cat Power, who I foolishly thought could be my friend one day, sings to us, **Dreams**.

I roll on top of Sam, making the first move, brushing his

soft, thick, dirty blonde hair back, and looking, photographing.

He looks so...real. I hope it's as safe and easy and as beautiful as

this, *next time, in the real world. Just, at least, thirty or forty years*

older, please.

"Follow my lead," I whisper.

An hour later, Sam and I are drinking Champagne and

toasting to what has turned out to be one hell of a prom night.

"I can go again," he offers.

"If I stay here with you, I'll never wake up. There's some

parallel lives shit going on tonight, Sam. I'm dreamer, remember?"

"So, I won you over with the **Deer Hunter**?" Sam asks.

"Well, there are many reasons, and that's one of them.

Your obscenely large penis was the clincher, however."

"You sound like a horny teenager," he teases.

"I am right now, aren't I?"

"I love **Deer Hunter**. Depressing and epic."

"That seems to be the party line, but that is not at all why I

love it."

"Then why do you like it?" he fishes.

"It's because of everything that's going on behind the

scenes."

"What happened *behind the scenes?*"

"The entire film is a testament to love. Meryl Streep only took the role because her lover, John Cazale, was in it and she wanted to be close to him as he was dying. And John was only in it, because Robert De Niro put up the insurance money and because he couldn't get insured. John was not predicted to make it through the filming alive, much less the release. John had played…"

"Fredo, in **The Godfather**," Sam says.

"Correct, with De Niro."

"Go on."

"John took the movie because he was an actor and being an artist is compulsive. To create is to be alive."

"That's a beautiful story."

I snort another line and start pacing the room, naked. So unlike me to be this confident with my body. *Very unlike my actual first time.* Like I said, *Magic Blow.*

"Tragic and beautiful. John was able to finish filming, but did not live to see the release. Meryl Streep nursed him. How kick ass is that? There's no greater act than caring for the sick. I've done it a few times, and I've never felt closer to Goddess."

"I will never think of the **Deer Hunter** the same way."

"But you want to know what really gets me about **Deer Hunter**? What really splits my chest open until my guts fall out like a fish? It's that long, goddam wedding scene. Every minute of it."

Sam snorts another line.

"Meryl's walking around for days on this movie set wearing a wedding dress thinking *I'm never going to marry John,* and John's thinking, *I'm never going to marry Meryl.* Their de facto wedding is on a disjointed movie set – *an alternative reality.* Have you ever heard of anything more heartbreaking? Yet they both manage to give great performances and are pieces to something larger than themselves – a great movie, a great piece of art."

"Holy fucking shit, is that deep. I don't know if I can handle this at eighteen – or on blow."

"I'm sorry, Sam. Art is never what it seems on the surface. There's *always* a back story. Tonight, I seem to be reliving mine."

"I think you might be the most romantic woman I've ever

met," he says. "It's like an *affliction* with you, *isn't it*?"

"You know, this was a great night, and don't take this the wrong way, but I didn't *need* it. I didn't even need to hear you tell me you loved me, although it sounded nice."

"I meant it."

"Question: is after sex talk always this intense?"

I start to laugh finally.

"No, it isn't, but you're with me, and I'm in the middle of an existential crisis and kind of lonely. Feel free to run out the door screaming if you need to. I swear I'm done with the serious talk."

"I like talking on this level, about ideas, but…"

"I'm sorry. At this age, you should only like a girl because she smells nice, or she lets you take naked pictures of her. No drama. When you're older, relationships can get much more complicated."

"Hey, can I take naked pictures of you?"

"I still look seventeen, right?"

"Yeah."

"Then, sure. What the hell?"

"Awesome!"

"And feel free to share them with all of your friends, *or on the internet,*" *I add.*

"I love you," he tells me again. I allow myself to believe him.

If I'm seventeen, then maybe my favorite radio station exists. It does - AM Thirteen Ninety. Sylvester's **You Make Me Feel (Mighty Real)** is on.

"Let's go clubbing!" I yell.

Sam and I are in the back of our limo hitting the Chicago nightlife with my VIP Club Cards in hand. All of the nightclubs of my youth are open. I know the DJs and the bouncers. Being underage will not be a problem!

We hit Jilly's and I let Sam do a line of Magic Blow off of my cleavage and we clank Long Island Iced Teas.

I hear cymbals up above on the speakers. Frankie Valli's **Can't Take My Eyes Off Of You.**

"**Deer Hunter!**" Sam yells.

I grab him by the arm out onto the dance floor.

"It's mandatory for Italian-Americans to get on the

dance floor when Frankie Valli is playing. I practiced my moves with Ne-Yo!"

"The wedding scene was not too long!" Sam yells at the top of his lungs.

"I know, it's perfect."

"Eddy, this is the greatest night of my life."

"So far, Sam. Wait till college."

"My jeans… they're different," he chuckles.

They're pleated… *and* French.

"Girbaud." I tell him, "I should give them to my friend David Duchovny. It's his life's quest to find the perfect pair of pleated pants."

Diana Ross' **I'm Coming Out** starts to play and my two nearly identical, gay, great-uncles arrive on the dance floor standing beside me in ironed Sergio Valente jeans and hairy chests covered in gold.

"I'm SO HAPPY!" I scream as they kiss my cheeks at the same time and we dance together joyfully. Alternate realities are the best! Ghosts too! They're always so nice to me! I love them!

We hit more bars, *Neo, The Bridge, Shelter*, till 5 am, and I notice we're running out of the *Magic Coke*. I imagine it will be gone by dawn.

One last thing.

We get back in the limo, drunk off our common youth; the idea of breaking through, *of new beginnings*.

The limo pulls up in front of our high school. We get out and walk onto the soccer field, hand in hand. I'm walking barefoot on the grass.

Sam throws his jacket on the dewy field and we both lie down and watch the sunrise. No music, no flashbacks, just the two of us, and the distant sound of the limo engine running on the street beside us.

He whispers:

I love you.

I whisper back:

I love you too.

It feels so good to say it. It feels so good to hear it.

I caress his face with my hand, pinch his lips with my fingers and slip my tongue inside of his mouth. *Seventeen.*

"You good?" I ask.

"Great," he answers.

"Did you read Thomas Stoppard's play, **The Real Thing,** in high school?" I ask.

"No. What's it about?"

"*Real* life takes place the same time a play is. Some of the characters are actors. It's about love. You're never quite sure what's the "real thing" and what's make-believe - you know, *the actual play?"* I explain.

"And this resonates because?"

"I'm not sure what *is* and *isn't* real anymore."

"You have issues with pleasure. You have issues with letting go," he says, as serious as dead Steve McQueen.

The limo honks from the street, breaking our silence. We pull ourselves up and start to walk toward it.

I let him get into the limo first. The door is still open.

"Where are you going?" he asks, reaching his hand out to grab mine.

"For a walk. I need to walk to clear my head - *to process.*"

"Thanks again," he says, looking slightly sad about having

to say goodbye.

"No…thank *you*," I say, smiling and slamming the door.

I walk East on Webster until I hit the Lincoln Park Zoo. I pass by the matte black seals and the Lion House. My father took my picture there once. Not one human to be found. I walk through the back entrance of the zoo and through the viaduct to Lake Michigan until I arrive at the North Avenue Beach. I pause in front of the old ship where white cement walls are chipping. I hear voices but it's deserted. It's where I used to meet my friends over summer vacation when I was ten. I wore a purple one piece and sprayed Sun In to bleach my hair. That summer, I memorized all the words to the Rolling Stone's song, **(I Can't Get No) Satisfaction.**

The sand is soft and the water is cold as I wade out into the water to my knees, beneath my leather dress, seeing a swan in the distance. It must have escaped from the zoo. Is this a message? From Steven Daedalus? Has tonight just been another episode in my own *Portrait of the Artist as A Nearly Fifty-Year-Old Woman?* Perhaps it's a dirty goose and not a swan. My vision's never been that great.

I walk back onto the sandy beach and sit down, sun rising. I notice that my once pleasantly plump hands are a little bonier and veined than before. Raised moles on my arms begin to disappear. *I must be changing back.*

I replay:

I love you.

and

I love you too.

I watch the waves to see if Marcello Mastroianni will emerge from the water.

I pull my phone and headphones out of my purse. Song 1 plays… *In Deep's* **Last Night a DJ Saved My Life.**

10 HAVE A WACKY WEDNESDAY

I wake up in ten thousand thread count Italian linens that smell like lavender. I feel well rested, as though the weight of the world's been lifted off my shoulders. I open my eyes and look beside me.

"Bonjour!" Guillaume Canet whispers to me, smiling a bright, beautiful and wrinkly smile.

I close my eyes again as I imagine...*I'm dreaming, right?* I open them.

"Don't be frightened," Guillaume tells me. "Today is your best day."

"Where am I?" I ask.

Guillaume kisses me. He tastes better than I remember.

169

When I open my eyes again, a sweaty Guillaume sleeps soundly on my bare chest and I try and figure out just where on Earth this beautifully decorated room I've found myself in *is*. Egon Schiele's **The Embrace** hangs above the dresser, under soft lights. Cindy Sherman's **Untitled Film Still #48** hangs between two large windows. Is it possible these are *orginals*? There are floor to ceiling bookshelves (with a ladder) reminiscent of Max Von Sydow's loft in Woody Allen's film, **Hannah and Her Sisters**.

I look out of the window and see the Empire State Building. I'm in New York. I live in a gorgeous apartment. I collect art. I'm dating Guillaume Canet. This is kind of wacky – like Dr. Suess's book, **Wacky Wednesday**.

I crawl out naked from beneath the sleeping Guillaume, tiptoeing in perfectly pedicured toes. I pass by a mirror on my way to the bathroom. I'm tiny. Is that... is that *my* body? I run into the bathroom and step on the scale. It says I am one hundred and fifteen pounds. I haven't weighed *this* since age ten. I'm five feet nine; that's like a size zero. How did this happen? I never wanted to be a size zero! I mean I joked about it, but I like my curves, love them. I have no butt! And where are my DDs?

Sophia Loren's going to make me get a boob job. I need something to calm my nerves - a Xanax, something; getting everything you want all at once can be scary. That's why it is supposed to take years; there needs to be a build-up. I open up the medicine cabinet and see rows of bottles with my name on the labels. Speed? Apparently, I'm *addicted* to speed. So that's how I got so skinny! Great. All I need before turning fifty is a trip to rehab.

A mobile phone in the bathroom rings. The caller ID says "Nikki Finke."

Nikki Finke is calling me? From "Deadline?"

"Hello." I answer.

"Eddy Sass. I need a statement from you. You're really starting your own movie Studio; just like Charlie Chaplin did at United Artists? You, Mindy Kaling, Amy Pohler and Tina Fey?" *I'm starting my dream all-female movie studio! NO WAY!*

The line beeps.

"Thanks, Nikki, gotta go, other line." I hang up with Nikki and click over. All I hear is screaming.

"What the fuck Eddy? Why haven't you signed this deal?" A man with a slight Chicago accent yells at me.

"Who the fuck are you?" I yell back.

"It's Ari, Eddy. Don't play dumb," an irate voice tells me.

"Ari who?" I ask, dumbfounded.

"Ari Emanuel, *you blue balling Dago bitch!* I'm your Agent, remember? How many amphetamines did you take this morning?"

"None. I'm off that shit." I tell him. *OMFG Ari Emanuel is my Agent?* I flush all of the pills down the toilet.

"This deal is worth a billion dollars. This all female run studio was the largest funding on Kickstarter, ever!"

"People actually want to fund my movies?"

"Yes, the movie, the books, the TV shows. You're starting your own network for Christ Sake. You've got Oprah scared. *Oprah!* See you tonight and don't make a scene!"

"See you where?" I ask.

"The **Tribeca Film Festival.** Hello. Your movie's premiering. My assistant's sending over some dresses for your interviews this afternoon. Don't be an asshole, Eddy. This is it." Ari tells me. *"This is what it feels like to finally make it."*

He hangs up.

I've made it, mother fuckers, I've made it!

Kiss my grits, Haters!

I open the bathroom door to find Guillaume standing there. He's bare chested and his pajama pants are hanging low. All I see are six-pack abs heading down to his groin. I gasp. He throws me face down on the bed.

"I don't know if I can stand, much less walk out of this room to do those interviews." I tell Guillaume. We both start laughing.

"You've made me feel *so* good. You have no idea. But, do I..." I begin to ask him, "...make *you* feel good?"

"Yes, very much." he tells me, grinning. "But I do miss your old body. From before you were so famous."

"You know, I don't," I begin, softly. "Please don't take it personally, you're wonderful, your energy, is wonderful."

He grabs my hand and squeezes it.

"I'm French. So, I know these things. I'm sure it will Happen," he reassures me.

I hate to break it to him that it won't.

God, he's gorgeous. I need to eat something.

"Oh, Goddess. I need to get ready for these interviews."

"You! Jump in the shower! I'll prepare breakfast! Fruit and coffee. And, just so you know, I've read all of your favorite books, watched all of your favorite movies and downloaded all of your favorite songs."

"You have? That's great but I want to learn about you, about what you love. I want you to teach me *new* things. *I like teachers.*"

This relationship isn't going to work -even in alternate reality.

I walk into the hot shower alone. What am I thinking? I walk down the hall to the kitchen, nearly slipping on the wood floors, and grab Guillaume to join me.

"None of the dresses fit!" I complain to the assistant, Kitty. I never thought that clothes being *too* big for me would ever be a problem. "I look ridiculous!"

"We'll just safety pin the back," she tells me.

"Fine. *Whatever,*" I relent as she pins me back into shape.

I look in the mirror and I hardly recognize myself. *Is this the person inside of me that I always wanted to come out? I mean, the girl I've kept at bay all of these years? I start to cry.*

"Oh, did I pinch? I am so sorry!"

"No, I'm fine. I've just waited so long for all of this. I thought it would never happen. Like it was just an alternate reality that I created in my head; to get me through day-to-day. But, its actually happening and with lightening quick speed, you know?"

"I don't know, *but I'm happy for you.*" She tells me, like she knows me or something.

An hour later, I find myself sitting on a stage that I'm sharing a couch with Kathie Lee Gifford and Hoda on **The Today Show**. I'm shaking. I think I'm going through speed withdrawal. I'm sweating through my dress and have a massive headache. I'm craving Swedish pancakes.

"So, Eddy, your movie is premiering tonight. How exciting! Did you always know Sofia Coppola would direct?" Hoda asks.

"No fucking (bleep) way. Sofia Coppola directed my film? Wow!" I say even though I'm cursing on television and apparently unaware of the details of my own film.

"Yes, they say she might win a Best Director for it," Hoda says.

"She should've won for **Lost In Translation** - but Hollywood has always been about dicks (bleep) before chicks."

Kathie Lee and Hoda continue to smile, *professionals*. I'm light headed.

"Guillaume Canet fucked (bleep) me so hard this morning that I can barely walk."

Kathie Lee and Hoda look concerned and try and change the subject.

"Okay, then, well, let's talk about your novel, ***Oedipa Sex?*** How did you come up with *that* ending? Remarkable! Is it true that it's been optioned as a film?" Hoda asks.

"I finished my novel, really?" I ask them, "I don't know *how it ended*... I've been stuck on it for months."

"Okay, well, good luck tonight at the premiere!" Kathie Lee says.

"Any last words you want to say to your fans?" Hoda asks.

"I think I might throw up."

"And, cut!" The Director yells.

I look down at my iPhone to see the text from Ari. "You dumb Dago Bitch."

Next stop: **Live with Regis and Kelly**.

Now this interview I'm pumped for. I adore Regis Philbin. He's the most successful Italian-American on television, and Kelly is a nice Dago girl from New Jersey. They should take good care of me, I hope. Please, let *Reege* jump up and down for me - please!

It's set break when I arrive, and I see Kelly sitting behind her desk. She's drinking a Stoli Splenda on the rocks out of a happy face mug with *Censorship is Blindness* printed on it and I ask "Hey, Kel. Where's Reege?"

"Didn't you know? Reege retired."

"WHAT? You're kidding me. I'm too late; too late to be interviewed by Regis Philbin? Nuts!"

"*He's actually a ghost,*" Kelly whispers.

"Oh, I love ghosts!" I say.

"Trying to clean your slate before your fiftieth birthday, huh?" Kelly asks.

"Yeah, how did you know?"

"I know everything about you, Eddy Sass. I'm a great TV Journalist, AND I'm literally inside your brain right now."

"So, who's replacing Reege?"

"We have fill-ins. Today, it's David Duchovny."

"No way! Are you serious?"

"Yes. He loves it here. I almost can't get rid of him. It's a relief when he's in LA. All he wants to do is talk about books. And I think he tries to trick me into looking dumb on television."

"Hello again, Eddy." I hear from a tall, slightly leering David Duchovny in his pompous, slightly effeminate New York accent. He smells like the Pacific Ocean. Goddam Princeton Grad Pescatarian.

"Oh, yes, David. Hello there." I answer, trying to act cool.

The production assistants move me on stage in between Kelly and David, behind a large desk. I'm nervous about the way I look now, the way I left things with David, that one, crazy, hash brownie filled night. I don't want to use the term, "soul mate" in a metaphysical sense, but he is.

"You've lost a lot of weight, Eddy. Nerves?" David asks.

"Oh, don't worry David. All I need is one, two weeks tops to gain twenty pounds back," I tell him, laughing. "How about you break your Vegan pledge and take me for a steak after this at Keen's?" I ask.

"Pescatarian," he corrects.

"Oh, yes, sorry, Pescatarian. No wonder you always smell so fishy."

"I'll take that as a compliment. All that fish oil keeps my skin smooth. Want to feel it?"

"It?"

"My skin."

"Oh, no."

"You're a Cinderella story, huh? Now, that you're the famous writer and filmmaker you always wanted to be, do you think you've suffered enough for your art to deserve this success? Don't you know there's a difference between famous and great?"

"Can't you just compliment me once? Just once! Is that so hard to do? Will your internal organs fail or something if you decide to actually say I have value?" I yell.

"Aren't I just a peon to you now?" he asks.

"Idiot- don't you know that having you and my art means getting everything that I've ever wanted?"

"You two know each other?" Kelly asks as if she's surprised.

"Well, we kind of have a connection. Am I right, David?

Or is it all just in my head?"

"Yes, Eddy, we have a connection. It's like you and I are old friends who love to bicker, who like to get under each other's skin and it's just a matter of time before one of us says *Screw it, let's just do this thing*. Am I right?"

"Sounds like the plot of a sitcom."

"My case. It got dismissed," he tells me. Looking right at me.

"Oh, good." I say, trying to get the words out. There are electric shocks running through my body.

"I'm off the meds," he says and grabs my hand and puts it in his lap.

"Action!" calls the Director and I'm stuck with the camera rolling, with my hand over David's quickly tightening pleated pants and making chit chat with my drunk muse, Kelly Ripa.

David just smiles and asks me some off-the-wall questions, taking pleasure in my awkwardness, pressing his hand down, *harder*, over my hand, in between his legs.

"Yep, Sofia Coppola, movie studio. All that Jazz." I answer David who I hate right now but want more than anything to kiss his sushi stained lips. David has that *indescribable thing* that's always been missing.

"Water. May I have some water, please?" I whisper.

"Well, alright then, good luck with the **Tribeca Film Festival** premiere tonight. Tell Bobby De Niro I say hi." Kelly says.

"And...*cut!*"

"Okay, I'm off to do an appliance commercial." Kelly slurs and leaves the desk.

David presses my hand down farther into his lap, like *he may even bruise me.*

"Well..." David asks, leering.

And then he flips me over his shoulders and carries me toward his dressing room.

"Duchovny, you bastard, let me down. I have another interview!" I scream.

Thank Goddess, I'm a size zero. I can enjoy this **Streetcar Named Desire** drama.

"Jon Stewart in an hour!" my assistant yells at me, right before David slams the door in her face.

David starts to unbutton his pleated pants and remove his shirt as I walk backwards toward the wall. He presses the play button on his tape deck and Sonic Youth's Carpenter's cover of

Superstar.

"Is this on a Playlist?" I ask.

"No, Mix Tape. I'm old fashioned," he answers.

"Title?" I ask, still walking backwards toward a wall in the

dark, enclosed space.

"*Projecting, Winter 2021*," he jokes as he walks toward me.

"I think you're right about that."

"I'm going to make a new one," he laughs. "It's called

Eddy's Big Orgasm, January."

"Wait, wait, wait. This is happening so fast." I rant, as

my limbs begin to shake. I can hardly speak, even my lips are

trembling.

"Shut up!"

"I'm in a serious relationship with the world's most

beautiful man, Guillaume Canet."

"I don't care," he says pushing me against a wall, my

hands keeping him at bay. "You don't love him. You love me."

"Why… why do you even want me?" I ask.

"Because I'm in your head, Eddy. Now all I want to do is

get in your pants. You just can't turn forty without..."

"Fifty," I say, *owning it.*

He kisses me.

"But, *I don't…*" I whisper, embarrassed.

He lifts me up in his arms and pushes me against the wall. He whispers Hebrew into my ear.

"Oh, Jewish Jesus, that's hot. Keep talking!" I yell.

I kiss him back excitedly; noticing a framed picture of a smiling Regis Philbin on the Tonight Show with Johnny Carson above the mirror across from our half naked bodies.

I'm about to have sex in Regis Philbin's old dressing room with David Duchovny. The last thing I see is a tattoo of Thomas Pynchon's Trystero Symbol on David's ass.

"I'm glad we met again," he tells me after, passing me a joint.

"I feel like such a slut right now, you have no idea." I confess.

"Ha, ha. I'm glad I'm such a good influence on you. I thought you said you wanted to be my *really big slut*?" He laughs.

"Did I say it, or think it? I'm getting confused."

"Does it even matter… here… right now?"

"Seriously, I just cheated on Guillaume. He's a good

man."

"A very good man you could care less about."

"Don't say that!"

"Connections are organic and elusive, Eddy. You can neither predict nor control them."

"It's nice to be surprised in life. To let things happen."

"How much time do you have before **The Daily Show**? Could I sully you further?" he asks.

"There's so much I want to talk to you about… that I think only *you* will understand. You've understood almost everything about me so far. Even when you're impotent, you're exceedingly attractive. You've proven that to me, yet another reason why I hate you," I say.

"Well, thanks for the compliment. If you're not hating me or threatening my life, I feel neglected."

"You get inside my head. You know that, David. I feel naked in your presence."

"Oooh, *I like that.* But all I really want to hear is that you're writing."

"Goddamit. you're deep, David! I just had a kid complain that my after-sex talk was too deep, but now that I'm with you, I remember how comfortable and safe I can feel."

"I'm not always deep. Remember I'm an actor? I'm putting you on most of the time."

"When I spent that night with you, it reminded me of **La Dolce Vita.** Not the film - *what Sophia taught me that it is."*

"Loren?"

"Yes, I know, it sounds ridiculous!"

"Not at all. I only expect the extraordinary from you, Eddy. When you put your mind to something, you make it happen."

"Sophia knows exactly what I want; *what makes me love someone."*

David reaches over and gives me a kiss.

"I say a lot of stupid shit." He smiles back at me.

"I know, I love that just as much as the witty things you say. I'm just sad because I know you only exist in my head."

"Everybody wants someone to know them, Eddy." David says, "It's the human condition. We're afraid that if something happens to us, we'll never have been known."

"Only romantics think that way," I argue.

"Well, you're a romantic, Eddy. It's one of the reasons I like you so much."

"Why did I ever think I was so special in wanting to be understood? Everybody wants that!"

"No, I didn't say everybody wants to be *understood.* Everybody wants to be *known.* Being understood is a completely different objective and one that only complicated, over-thinkers torture themselves over; *those who are in the midst of an existential crisis.*"

"Like *me*." I say.

"Like *you*. But that's why I like you. *That's why I love you*. You're *complicated*."

"Tonight – this quest – *that's an understatement.*"

We both start belly laughing.

Enter uncomfortable pause.

"I'm glad I got to see *that*," David says, seriously, looking deep into my eyes and forcing a fight or flight response.

"What?" I answer.

"Don't be coy after nearly deafening my left ear with your screams."

"I didn't even put that on my list; didn't think it possible. An earthquake. What do you want me to say – thank you?"

"*Thank you, sir* would be better."

"Thank you, sir," I answer.

"Maybe this birthday will be the start of something new. Not just professionally."

"Why? Didn't it happen sooner? When I was still young?" I ask.

"All that matters is that it *can* happen. You had to let go of a lot of anger to let it happen. So many things you want can *still* happen Eddy. Trust me. You trust me, don't you? If you didn't, *that* wouldn't have just happened."

"But you and I - we'll never be together, never be a couple?" I whine.

"It's like you said, I'm unavailable. I'm the person you need to believe exists." He says. "I do exist. I do."

"It helps that I only thought of you, when I was with you." I add. I didn't drift off. I was present.

"That's how it should be. Hey, I'll miss you, you know?"

"None of this seems real except for that pounding you just gave me."

We laugh. He kisses my forehead. He has a sweet side to him. He's not *all* cock-sucking, Ivy League, pedantic bastard.

"Want another hit before you go?" he asks.

"I don't want to be too stoned before I meet Jon Stewart." I answer.

"Listen, everybody on that set is stoned," he tells me.

I put my clothes back on. David just lies on the couch, watching.

"So, how much longer till your birthday?" he prods.

"What time is it?"

"Four o'clock."

"Then, that would be eight more hours," I answer as I place my foot into a heel.

"I'm having my movie premiere at the **Tribeca Film Festival**, Ari Emanuel is my agent, I'm dating the world's most beautiful man, I'm starting my own film studio, and I just you-know-what with David Duchovny."

"You-know-what with David Duchovny?"

"Well, you know…" I say.

"I know. And I've got the scratch marks on my back to prove it."

"I guess I've done it all. What else could I possibly do before tomorrow? I've dealt with pretty much everything. Might make a good book one day."

I kiss Duchovny on the cheek, throw my coat on and follow my assistant to the next studio.

Next Stop: **The Daily Show**

"You're here to discuss your upcoming book – *Oedipa Sex,"* My assistant reminds me.

"But, I haven't even finished it. The last story is still being written; it's still happening, *like right now,*" I tell her.

"Jon's a nice guy. Just don't let him suck you into politics. He'll *crush you like a bug*." She warns me.

"I hate politics," I tell her.

"Keep that to yourself," she warns.

I'm moved up to the interview desk to a smiling Jon Stewart. I wish David was with me. He's so good at witty comebacks. My lips keep sticking to my teeth. I have the munchies.

"And, roll 'em!" The Director shouts.

"And we're back!" Jon begins to the studio audience, "Today, we have a writer and filmmaker *extraordinaire.* About to head the *first ever* female run film studio. Her first feature film, **Not My Girlfriend,** is premiering tonight at the **Tribeca Film Festival** and she's about to publish a new book called **Oedipa Sex.**

Please give a warm round of applause for *Eddy Sass*!"

The applause is so loud. Is that for me?

"So let's talk about your book." Jon says. "What happens to the Protagonist in the end?"

"I don't know, Jon. *I just don't know.* I'm not even sure what we're talking about anymore. *I'm exhausted from fucking hot men all day.* These stage lights are hurting my eyes. Do you have any Visine? Fritos? *Tab?"*

Next step on my itinerary is the **Tribeca Film Festival**. My assistant undresses and dresses me while I take a nap. The price to pay to work your way up the ladder in Hollywood. I guess she's my minder. She had some good luck with the TV actor Kiefer Sutherland, back in the day, so they sent her to me. Apparently, I have a reputation for being a bitch who's hopped up on speed.

When I wake up in the limo, I try and thank my hard working assistant, Kitty, but before I have a chance, she sticks a straw attached to a giant iced Americano into my mouth. I drink and start to wake up. Guillaume sits across from me, speaking to

Kitty in French. They sound like a Stereolab song.

When I finish the Iced Americano, he hands me a Kir - my favorite!

"I remember when my first film had its premiere," he says.

He's so good looking, this Guillaume. I keep forgetting what a talented actor, writer and filmmaker he is. I mean he won a French Oscar!

"How did it feel?" I ask him, smiling.

"Scary. I mean it's scary having your dream come true. People are going to watch and judge you. I don't know how one idea in your head becomes a film, or a book, but it does."

"Guillaume, this whole day has been kind of scary. I've always felt like I was on the verge of something great. Always on the verge, and now I am actually IN IT? Do you get what I'm saying?"

"Yes, *you have to be it* – not just wish it, and you've done it!"

"But, I haven't even seen the film yet, and I poured my heart and soul into that script. What if it's terrible?" I ask.

"Then you laugh and laugh. This film will always be perfect in your mind."

"You're right, it will be. I often forget when I'm hypnotized by your smile, just how smart you are, how talented you are. I'm a lucky woman, being your girlfriend. Even if it's only for one magical day."

"I told you - the best day ever!"

The limo pulls up onto the red carpet. That's right bitches! I'm walking the red carpet to my very own film premiere. Bobby De Niro is at the end of it and the world's most beautiful man is on my arm. Sofia Coppola directed my film!

Guillaume charms everyone in my wake. I'm a nervous wreck - all the flashbulbs going off in my face - and the anemia from the giant weight loss I just endured is making me feel faint. I see Ari Emanuel at the end of the red carpet waiting for me. He's pointing to his watch. No other than Marky Mark – aka Mark Wahlberg - is standing beside him. Motherfucker is short but cute. My Dad used to hustle pool with a guy named Boston Shorty. *Mark's got a new nick-name.*

"Hi, I'm Eddy." I say to Marky Mark, "Nice to meet you."

"It's nice to finally meet you, Eddy. I'm the star of your movie."

"WHAT!? How did that happen? Ari!"

"Suck it, Eddy, because it's a great movie. Mark is great in it and he even raps."

"What!?!? At no point should Marky Mark, I mean *Boston Shorty* - rap in my film!"

"Boston Shorty?" yells Ari.

"This is why I only make movies in France," Guillaume confides.

"Just watch the damn thing and smile," Ari tells me. "Enjoy that you've made it. I mean, isn't it your birthday tomorrow?"

"At midnight, yes," I answer.

"Then, lighten the fuck up. I've got calls to make." Ari yells and walks out of the theater. I swear, with that mouth, he grew up in the pool room with me.

I sit beside Guillaume in the front row of the theater and Sofia Coppola sits a few seats in front of me.

Guillaume holds my hand as the opening credits roll for my film, **Not My Girlfriend.**

"I'm glad it turned out so well," Sofia says, over Champagne at the after party.

"You know, I always wanted to be just like you. You were kind of my Italian-American role model," I say.

"Thanks. I'm grateful I get to do this for a living," she says.

"You should be. Today is kind of my **Wacky Wednesday**. All of this success is hard for me to believe, and I have a sinking suspicion that when I wake up tomorrow, my regular life will just go back to normal."

"It doesn't have to be," Sofia whispers into my ear and it's like I'm Scarlett Johanssen and she's Bill Murray in the final scene of **Lost in Translation.**

I walk toward Guillaume and Marky Mark who are checking sports scores on their iPhones.

"Well, Mark, you pulled it off. It wasn't exactly what I'd imagined, but you did it. Thank you for being in my movie."

"Why so blue?" Guillaume asks. "I liked the movie a lot."

"Thank you, thank you, Guillaume." I tell him and touch his face with my hand. I need reassurance that he's real. I start to cry.

"Please, please don't cry. Don't cry my darling," he says as he calms me by holding me and stroking my hair.

"This isn't really happening, is it? Either that or this starvation diet is making me edgy. The only way I can have this happiness, this pleasure, this success, is in my dreams. I'm a dreamer. I know this."

"It all starts with dreams," Guillaume whispers.

"I'm having the time of my life - just pretending all of my dreams came true. I'm sad to see it all end."

Guillaume kisses my forehead. He feels bad for me right now. It hurts him to see me this way – he's a part of me. I invented him.

"I think I should go to the ladies' room and freshen up." I excuse myself and head to the powder room. It's an old fashioned one with Louis IVI chairs that are covered in pink velvet. I pat my face with powder. I try and focus on my face in the mirror, but my image gets blurry. I've always found it hard to focus on my image in a mirror while I am dreaming. I look at the clock. It's ten o'clock. Only two more hours before I turn fifty, before this dream comes to an end.

The door to the powder room opens. It's David Duchovny. *again.*

"David, what are you doing here? I like to have my

nervous breakdowns all by myself, thank you," I say, trying to push him out the door.

I grab David's wrist tightly, squeezing it. I need to feel his pulse so that I know I'm still in the dream, *that it's all still happening...*

"Okay, Okay, I'm sorry. Just come with me. I want to take you somewhere."

He holds me while I calm down and then I hold his hand and walk out of the powder room and the movie theater and onto a quiet, New York street. There's a car waiting. I get in the car and David is beside me.

Leonard Cohen's **Suzanne** begins to play.

"David!"

"Shhh!." he interrupts. "It's a beautiful song and reminds you of a beautiful time in your young life. *There are still new beginnings.*"

"I hope so, David. I need to believe it to be true."

I see we are heading to midtown - Rockefeller Center.

We head up the elevator. The doors open and we arrive at the Rainbow Room at the top of the Rockefeller Center. I hear Blondie's **Pretty Baby** playing in the distance. I pass by a mirror to look at myself. My hair is bleached blonde with black tips. I'm wearing a spaghetti strap, white silk dress and high heeled, white flip flops with a white band around my arm. I'm Blondie, from the cover of the **Parallel Lines** album.

"Whoa!" I ask David, "What's happening?"

"You can be anyone you want to be tonight," he snickers. "It's like CBGBs all over again!"

I look on stage, and there's a young Debbie Harry, and we're dressed exactly the same. Her band is on stage; perhaps a ghost or two. I hear her sing a line about **La Dolce Vita**.

"They're playing for you," David tells me. "You wore a Blondie button on your jean jacket as a tween. You played the album **Parallel Lines** at slumber parties."

"I like the idea of **Parallel Lines**," I say.

"Yeah, I guess so."

I walk through the candlelit room with the marvelous views of nighttime New York on all sides. It's a birthday party - for me. Prince is in a booth drinking a Yoo-hoo.

"He might just play some dirty songs for you later," David announces.

Penny, my Sorority Doppelganger, and her boyfriend

Chase are giggling on the dance floor. Chan Marshall is handing out Elephant Buttons. Ne-Yo is in deep conversation with the ghost of James Lipton. R. Kelly is showing his bejeweled handgun to Little Bertha who is dressed as Ronald Reagan and is also carrying a fire arm. Sophia Loren and Marcello Mastroianni are on the dance floor, embracing. Guillaume, Ari and Marky Mark are chowing down on Steak Frites and betting on the Knicks game. Sam Schulman, my prom date, is dressed in a tuxedo, filming Catherine Deneuve who can never say no to a camera in her face or a cigarette. "So cool," he whispers to me.

The ghosts of Serge Gainsbourg and Steve McQueen are hitting on the cocktail waitresses.

"This, is amazing, David. Thank you. I'm speechless."

"If you're speechless, then I know I've done a good job. Now, get up on that stage and sing!"

I hear an impressive drum solo. The Blondie song **Dreaming** begins.

"Get up there right now!" David yells and I nearly trip, climbing up to the stage to sing my favorite Blondie song; my favorite song about...life; with a young and magnificent Debbie Harry. I'm sure they turned off my microphone, but I'll still sing as loud as I can.

My heart flutters as I allow myself this surge of pleasure, in case this quest, these crazy dreams, are in fact coming to an end at midnight.

David dances; he's happy for me, happy for my night. He's a really bad dancer, but he makes me feel young and free. *I wish he was my best friend!*

I look over into the audience and see Kim Gordon and Thurston Moore of *Sonic Youth* walk up to the front of the audience. They look twenty years younger. They wave to me, up on stage and hold hands and smile. Ne-Yo points to them and gives me a thumbs up. Kim and Thurston are back together; even if only for this one night.

"This party, what a send-off!" I cry out.

"*Sonic Youth* is up next, don't go too far. **Teenage Riot** on Deck!" David yells.

"Um, greatest… night…of… my… life. Thank you. Thank you." I'm not angry and I don't feel guilty or scared or ashamed of being me. This is another *first*. I've been stripped bare, to my creamy Hostess cupcake vanilla filling. I let it go. *I let it all go.*

"Don't, you know, forget all of us, when you wake up.

When this dream is over."

"So this has all just been a dream? Figures."

"We're always here for you, you know, if you need us. We're all rooting for you."

"I love and will miss all of you. I don't know if I've ever had this much fun! I feel so good!" I howl.

I look at the clock. It's eleven. One hour left until my birthday.

"One more surprise!' David tells me and drags me to another booth. And there they are – my parents! They're exactly as I remember them as a little girl – glamorous celebrities. My mother is wearing a blue silk dress, gold earrings and the emerald and diamond ring that she sold to help pay for my tuition. I can smell her signature Joy perfume. *The most expensive in the world, she said.*

"Happy Birthday, Princess," my Mother says.

"Happy Birthday, Angel," my Dad says.

I think I need to reread Tom Stoppard's play, **The Real Thing.**

"I've been wasting a lot of time pretending I'm someone else, haven't I?" I say.

"Just *be* her already, and stop *pretending!*" My Dad yells.

"I've always been an artist in your eyes, haven't I?" I ask

"Yes," my parents say in unison.

"Every day, with you as our daughter, was magical," my mother says. I want the three of us to crawl under a warm blanket and stay there. I need their love so much. I miss it. Some days, I feel lost without them. I feel lost without feeling loved and special. That my existence means something - *I make two people happy because I'm their work of art.*

"As you know, I have dreams within my dreams. In this one, I had three sons. One of them was learning to ride a bike for the first time and I was going to teach him to ride it up a hill. Once you reached the top, there was a plateau and you could rest. There were other accomplished bikers waiting at the top. To reach the top was a small feat, but a feat nonetheless. I biked up that hill with my son, hoping he would make it, hoping I would make it... *make it to the top.* Those last few pedals that finally got you to the plateau were the hardest, the most exhausting. But I pushed through and made it to the top and my son made it to the top. We accomplished something major and the view from the top of the hill was beautiful, and I realized that I always gave up on that last push. You know, the last push to the top of the hill? I always let something drag me down; like my odd family, lack of money, a lack of confidence, or someone else's opinion stand in my way. Those last ten pedals. That's what makes the difference in getting or not getting what you want – when you overcome your fears and believe you can do something you've never done before. You find the strength and the belief in yourself and you just do it. I'm ready for that last push to get what I want. I'm inspired by these adventures. *When I wake up from this dream, this wonderful, wonderful dream."*

"It's almost midnight, Eddy," Duchovny says and grabs my hand.

I hug and kiss my parents, not wanting to let go.

"Oh, darling, we're always with you," my Mother says.

"Believe in ghosts," my Dad says, grinning.

"I do," I say back. "Only good ones."

"Sorry, *things happen fast in alternate realities,"* David reminds me and starts to walk me out of the ballroom. We stop at the elevator doors.

"It's hard to find a best friend," I stutter, choking back tears. He takes me in his arms and I relax into his strong and warm

embrace. *I made it through my quest; I made it through the night.*

I open my eyes, happy and sad, and look into his - bold

blue and reassuring - *as the lights dim and his face turns into my*

own.

11 MORNING

Oedipa woke up at home, in her own bed, thirsty, yet with the urge to pee, with The Kinks' **She's Got Everything** playing on the radio.

On the floor, she sees her laptop, almost screaming at her, with stories she's no longer afraid to share.

It's her birthday.

She feels tingles. Good ones. Real ones. Electric. Is it? Is it possible? *Dr. Frankenstein?*

She jumps out of bed and pulls the drapes apart, admiring the sunlight pouring in. She rips off all of her clothes *like her own lover would,* not caring if her neighbors see her.

I'm an exhibitionist!

Taking a deep breath, standing in front of her full length mirror, she puts her right hand over her heart, savoring every delightful beat and greets her reflection in the mirror with a smile.

This is me.

And I love her.

PLAYLIST

PRINCE	*BLUE LIGHT*
	LITTLE RED CORVETTE
	KISS
	EROTIC CITY
SHEILA E.	*A LOVE BIZARRE*
VANITY 6	*NASTY GIRL*
APPOLLONIA 6	*SEX SHOOTER*
PRINCE	*BALLAD OF DOROTHY PARKER*
	IT
	SLOW LOVE
	ADORE
	HEAD
	SOMETIMES IT SNOWS IN APRIL
	SEXY M.F.
X	*THE WORLD'S A MESS, IT'S IN MY KISS*
HARRY NILSSON	*EVERYBODY'S TALKING*
DIANE KEATON	*SEEMS LIKE OLD TIMES*
LIL' TROY	*WANNA BE A BALLER*
CYPRESS HILL	*INSANE IN THE BRAIN*
BILLIE HOLIDAY	*LOVE ME OR LEAVE ME*
VELVET UNDERGROUND	*I FOUND A REASON*
CAT POWER	*THE GREATEST*
MARCIA GRIFFITHS	*ELECTRIC BOOGIE (THE ELECTRIC SLIDE)*
R KELLY	*STEP IN THE NAME OF LOVE*
	(TRAPPED) IN THE CLOSET
	BUMP N' GRIND
	HAPPY PEOPLE
	TRAPPED IN THE CLOSET
NE-YO	*CLOSER*
DJ CASPER	*CHA CHA SLIDE*
TODD RUNDGREN	*I SAW THE LIGHT*
SONIC YOUTH	*TEENAGE RIOT*

D'ANGELO	*UNTITILED (HOW DOES IT FEEL)*
STEREOLAB	*MISS MODULAR*
	CYBELE'S REVERIE
	PERCOLATOR
SERGE GAINSBOURG	*RELAX BABY BE COOL*
NEW ORDER	*TEMPTATION*
SONIC YOUTH	*MOIST VAGINA*
ROXY MUSIC	*OVER YOU*
CAT POWER	*STILL IN LOVE*
	DREAMS
SYLVESTER	*YOU MAKE ME FEEL (MIGHTY REAL)*
FRANKIE VALLI AND THE FOUR SEASONS	
	CAN'T TAKE MY EYES OFF OF YOU
DIANA ROSS	*I'M COMING OUT*
ROLLING STONES	*(I CAN'T GET NO) SATISFACTION*
INDEEP	*LAST NIGHT A DJ SAVED MY LIFE*
SONIC YOUTH	*SUPERSTAR*
LEONARD COHEN	*SUZANNE*
BLONDIE	*PRETTY BABY*
	DREAMING
THE KINKS	*SHE'S GOT EVERYTHING*

OEDIPA SEX

ABOUT THE AUTHOR

Catherine Adami is the author of *On Elizabeth Street* (2016), a novel set in NYC's Nolita. A Chicago native, Cat has a B.A. from Tulane University in History. Known as The Pool Hustler's Daughter, Cat can be found reading at Open Mikes in both Chicago and NYC. She's currently writing a memoir, *Cool Parents*.

OEDIPA SEX